AUTHOR CLARKE - A	CLASS No. F C
TITLE A MIND TO MURDER	BOOK No. 87107431

A MIND TO MURDER

This is not so much a detective novel as a serious (and utterly convincing) study of the seeds and inexorable growth of a crime. It concerns a psychiatrist, his ex-actress wife, his son Richard – a student, and his crippled daughter, Caroline. The action begins when an orphaned relation, Janet, comes to stay with the family: Richard falls in love with her, Caroline's jealousy looks as if it might blossom into hideous violence.

A MIND
TO MURDER

By

Anna Clarke

1971
CHATTO & WINDUS
LONDON

Published by
Chatto & Windus Ltd
40 William IV Street,
London W.C.2

*

Clarke, Irwin & Co Ltd
Toronto

BR/BR.

ISBN 0 7011 1665 x
© 1971 Anna Clarke

Printed in Great Britain
by Cox & Wyman Ltd.,
London, Fakenham and Reading

To
BELINDA

A MIND TO MURDER

I

My sister Caroline spends her life in a wheelchair. She is nineteen years old and five years ago she had polio, which left her unable to walk. She can prop herself upright for a few moments provided she has something firm to cling to and can just manage to drag herself along for a foot or two. This doesn't sound much, but in fact it is very important because it means she can go to the lavatory and wash and get to bed by herself. Either my mother or Mrs Dring, our cleaning woman, helps her to have a bath and for the rest she moves about the flat in her chair, which she is very clever at manœuvring.

The greatest problem is getting her back and forth to college, where she is reading for a degree in maths. I take her to lectures whenever I can – I am two years older than she is and am in my last year reading chemistry – but other times she has to be dependent upon help from other students or from my mother. She feels this badly, and we are hoping that eventually she may be able to have an invalid carriage, but at the moment the problems of parking and finding someone to help her out make it rather too complicated.

We moved house after her illness and are on the ground floor of a block of flats in North London. It's on a busy road, and has not much of an outlook in front, and it backs straight on to a stretch of canal with railway sidings beyond; but the big rooms and wide doors make it easy for Caroline and, above all, there is only a very shallow step down to the pavement. Caroline has found a way of bumping her chair down this so that she can get out of the block by herself. She goes to the pillar-box at the corner and even a little way farther where there is a small public garden. She has to wait, though, for someone to help her up the step again when she comes back.

But at least it means that she has one little corner of life that she can call her own, and my father and I never ask her who she has seen or what she has done in the gardens unless she starts telling us first. My father is consultant psychiatrist at St Martin's Hospital and although I don't think he is always very wise in his attitude towards Caroline, at least he does appreciate her need for this minimal piece of freedom. Unfortunately my mother doesn't seem to understand, or perhaps it is simply that she can't control her anxiety, because she is always trying to prevent Caroline going out by herself and always tries to subject her to an inquisition on her return. Dad and I usually win, though, because Mother is fundamentally rather old-fashioned in her outlook and tends to defer to the male members of the family. She is also somewhat afraid of Caroline, as indeed we all are.

My sister was clever enough even before she became ill, but since her paralysis everything that is in her seems to have become concentrated in her willpower and her intellect. I believe she cares more for me than for anyone else in the world, but there are times when I catch her looking at me in a way that makes my blood run cold and I can see she is bitterly envious of my freedom and my prospects, and that for all her affection for and dependence on me, she would at such moments wish me to come to grief. She used to be jealous of me even when we were young children and I think this was Mother's fault. My father is outwardly much the stronger partner in the marriage, but it is odd how an apparently docile person can in fact set the tone for a situation, and what I think happened was that we grew up being quite unconsciously influenced by Mother's attitude that it was the boy who mattered and the girl's role was to be domestic and inferior. I suppose I took advantage of it, which is hardly surprising, particularly since I have always known in my heart that Caroline had much the better brains and that I would never be anything more than an average plodder.

At any rate all this changed after Caroline's illness and resulted in Mother making herself a slave to the three of us, although Dad and I do help as much as she lets us, and I would certainly have gone to a university away from home and had a more normal sort of student life if it hadn't been for Caroline. However, I can't complain too much because even now I manage to get quite a lot of time away from it all and it's only a question of hanging on until I get my degree, after which I'm going to look for a job away from home.

It would have been different if I had been another girl. Heaven help any sister of Caroline's! She would have been made an even worse slave to Caroline than my mother is; she would have been made to feel guilty every moment of her life; she would have borne the full brunt of Caroline's jealousy and frustration.

That was what the situation was like in our home when my father suggested that my cousin Janet should come to live with us after her parents had been killed in a car crash. It was Sunday lunch-time, and we were just coming to the end of the usual huge meal.

'I think we ought to offer to give the child a home, Phyllis,' he said. 'She hasn't any other close relatives except that old cousin of her father's who isn't a suitable person at all.'

Mother jumped at the idea. 'Poor child, poor little

Jan – she's only seventeen, you know. I'd been hoping you might want to do this – poor child. I've been wondering all along what on earth she was going to do – Margery would have wished it, I'm sure, and she'll be company for Caroline, won't she, darling?'

Mother turned to her anxiously, but Caroline sat there with her deadpan expression and said nothing.

'Yes, yes,' said my father impatiently and I could guess what he was thinking. 'She won't be at home much of the time, though. She will have to take a job to pay for her keep as soon as she's fit. We don't want her to feel she is here on charity and besides, after an experience like that it will be much better if she keeps herself busy.'

'And what sort of occupational therapy do you propose, Daddy?' asked Caroline, stretching out a hand to take another banana.

I pulled the bowl away and said: 'That's your limit. I knew you'd never stick to that diet.'

She made a face at me, although in fact she likes us to bicker a little occasionally because it makes her feel more like other girls. 'Are you going to put her nose to the grindstone the moment she comes out of hospital?' she asked. 'Poor cousin Janet indeed.'

'Not the very moment,' said my father calmly. 'She has had severe concussion as well as other injuries and will obviously need a further period of rest. But she has learnt shorthand and typing, and as Matron's secretary is leaving in a few weeks' time, there will be a vacancy at St Martin's if she cares to take it.'

'Pure nepotism,' said Caroline, greedily chewing her banana. 'Won't it put her in a rather invidious position *vis-à-vis* the other staff?'

'Don't you think that would be asking rather too much of her, Andrew dear?' said my mother. 'Don't you think it might be better to let her potter around for a few months first and then take a little part-time job? She could come shopping with me and go out with Caroline sometimes. Janet never was much of a career girl. Margery always used to say so.'

'If she comes to us she is going to do a proper job. And lead a normal sort of life. I'm not having the girl brought into this household to be made a domestic drudge.'

There was a silence after this. I'm afraid my father hasn't got the sweetest of tempers and my mother always manages to exacerbate it. At any rate it put a stop to the subject, for which I was grateful, because I thought the whole idea was daft and I was determined to tell my parents so, although I wanted to sound out Caroline first.

I thought I knew her pretty thoroughly, but she reacted in a totally unexpected way.

'Why shouldn't Janet come and live with us?' she said as if it was a matter of complete indifference to her. 'The child has nowhere else to go. It'll give Mother someone else to fuss over and as far as I can remember she's a poor little mousy thing and is hardly likely to interfere with our activities.'

'Now then, Carol.' We had gone into her room; I'd helped her on to the bed for her afternoon's rest and I kept an arm around her. 'It's no use pretending this doesn't matter. It matters a lot. You've got to be honest. It's only a suggestion and if we say we don't like it they'll change their minds. Would you like Janet to come and live here, or wouldn't you?'

She gave an affected yawn. 'Really, Dickie' – she calls me this when she's feeling affectionate or when she's determined to be obstructive, usually the latter – 'the whole thing is too much in the air to take so seriously. The girl may not want to come. Or even if she does, she seems to be the type who would have plenty of boys in tow. She'll be getting married in five minutes.'

There was no bringing her round to discussing it sensibly: she'd pulled the blinds down – snap. If even I can't talk to Caroline when she is in that mood, then certainly no one else can. But it worried me far more than if she had reacted either with alarm or with a false enthusiasm and I was more determined than ever to try to prevent Janet's coming. I couldn't decide which of my parents was likely to be more easily worked on so I decided to tackle them together. I found them in Dad's consulting-room, where he usually reads and writes on Sunday afternoons. Mother had followed him there and was already having a go at him.

'Please don't be too hard on Janet, dear. She's very young and she's had a terrible shock and she may not be up to Matron's standard of work at all for all you know – it's all very well for you clever people, but you don't always understand what it's like for people who find things difficult.'

'Please, Phyllis, please allow me to know what I'm doing. I am not entirely inexperienced in the varieties of human capabilities.'

'No, dear, no, of course not. All those peculiar patients of yours. But after all, this is my own sister's child, and it's not as if she's clever like Caroline and I must say I do feel that you expect too much even from Caroline sometimes —'

She broke off then because they had both noticed I had come in. I stepped forward.

'Dad, I don't think Janet ought to come here at all.'

I didn't mean it to sound so abrupt and high-handed, but the fact is that I'm a little bit in awe of my father and sometimes it bursts out in this rather infantile defiance, which makes me furious with myself and that only makes it worse.

'Really?' he said in his most Olympian manner. 'And why, in your wisdom, have you decided that?'

'Because it's not fair on her – because we're not the sort of household for a normal girl to live in – because it'll be difficult with Caroline. I mean, Janet's a pretty little thing and there are bound to be tensions —'

I went floundering on. They both stared at me.

'Am I to take it, Richard,' said my father at last, 'that you feel yourself personally in danger of succumbing to Janet's charms and consequently of arousing jealousy in Caroline? Are you really so susceptible? Haven't you other sources for gratifying your need for female favours?'

I wanted to go through the floor. Every now and then Dad gets at me like this. I know father–son relationships are notoriously difficult, but one would think that in the case of an eminent psychiatrist . . . however, I suppose he has to have so much patience with crazy people during his working life that he feels he must let fly a bit and relax at home, but I find it terribly hard to take and it doesn't help much to think of Caroline's explanation, which is that my father is fundamentally jealous of me. He is absolutely faithful to my mother, we are sure, but Caroline thinks that he sees me as having all sorts of wild affairs that he can't have himself. She may be right, but I hate thinking about it and in any case I don't have so very many affairs at all and I always fade out quietly if I feel somebody is getting serious, because there is going to be a hell of a struggle with Caroline when I do marry and there's no point going through a lot of unnecessary preliminary skirmishes. She knows I have never been serious over anybody and in fact we make a sort of a joke of it, which makes me feel rather mean towards the girl in question, but it does help my relationship with Caroline.

'It isn't because of me at all,' I said to my father. 'What I meant was that any girl who comes to live here with Caroline is going to feel wretched about her all the time. Unless she's a completely insensitive egoist and Janet isn't that. Far from it.'

'I'm sure Caroline would be kind to her,' said my mother. 'She knows what a bad time Janet has been through. It might make her feel protective towards her. Wouldn't it be good for Caroline to feel she could look after somebody else a bit?' My mother looked at Dad anxiously and didn't sound very convinced by what she was saying. 'You're always telling me I have to let her be independent,' she went on, 'and not treat her like a child.'

My father muttered something impatiently and I couldn't make out which side Mother was really on in the discussion. She had sounded extremely keen on the idea, but it was just conceivable that that was a blind and that she was really trying to get my father to drop it but wanted him to think he had dropped it of his own accord. That might have been the reason why she was making all these irritating remarks about having Janet in the house; they might have been intended as a sort of forewarning to my father of what he might expect if Janet came. I couldn't be bothered, however, with this roundabout business of hers, and there was obviously no point in my saying anything more to him. We'd got into one of those beastly family tangles where there is no way out at all and you are lucky if you can run away.

I had been intending to do some reading, but suddenly I had an overwhelming longing to be out of the flat. I went straight round to Lesley's place, and luckily she was in and very willing to waste a few hours too, and by the time I got home again I felt refreshed and had things rather more in proportion.

I always feel vaguely uneasy when I come into our flat after being away from it for some hours. It is rather dark, since the road is not very wide and there is a high block opposite, and although it is always kept clean and well decorated and we have perfectly good modern furniture, it never feels light and cheerful but has an oppressive atmosphere rather like a dentist's waiting-room. Of course my father does see some patients at home and they are usually pretty bad mental cases so they may add to the feeling, but it isn't only that. My friend Brian's father is a doctor too, and they have far more coming and going of patients than we have, but I have never felt there that heavy gloomy feeling that I always do when I come home. Perhaps it comes from having a disabled person in the place, but there again I've been in people's homes where there's been really serious illness and still the atmosphere has been brighter and more hopeful. It's not that we are all of us always miserable and quarrelsome. Dad can be most entertaining when he is in the right mood, and that sparks Mother off, and as for Caroline, considering what she has to put up with, she really complains very little. But I think it must be something to do with Caroline, because whatever we are doing, whatever we are talking about, we are never able to forget for one instant that she is hopelessly paralysed. She is never able to accept it but is weighed down with resentment and frustration at all times and it hangs over the lot of us like a pall. It is as if there were five of us living in the flat – Mother and Dad and myself and Caroline, and the constant menacing presence of Caroline's disability.

This all sounds very fanciful for somebody who is mainly concerned with scientific facts and discipline as I am, but after all, one is bound to be influenced by one's parentage, and you need quite a lot of perception to be a good psychiatrist, while as for my mother, she was an actress before her marriage and always claims to be very sensitive to atmosphere. Sometimes I wonder whether she isn't putting on an act all the time with this fussy domesticity; there's an unexpectedly sharp tone of voice sometimes and a very straight look in the eye, and it may be that she's laughing at the lot of us. It's rather fashionable among my crowd at the moment to analyse our parents and it may be that I am letting my imagination run away with me, but I am not just imagining this depressing feeling about my home. I know that some visitors sense it, and Mrs Dring once confessed to me that it affected her too, but she is such a nice old body that she seems to dispel it when she potters around cleaning.

Janet felt it, I'm sure, the moment she came into the hall.

My parents had gone to collect her from King's Cross, having decided that it would be more appropriate for them to go than for me to. It was a Sunday afternoon in late February and there had been continuous snow and slush on the ground for several weeks, which had deprived Caroline of her own little independent venture outside. She was in one of her strangest moods, partly because of being shut up for so long and partly, I am sure, because of Janet's coming, although she had taken it very calmly when it had finally been decided and had made very little comment on it since.

The small guest-room next to the consulting-room at the front of the flat had been made ready for Janet. This was at my insistence, my mother having originally suggested that Janet should take over my room next door to Caroline's, 'since it would be nice for the two girls to be near each other'. Caroline had laughed out loud at this, with genuine amusement, but a moment later she had said in her most quietly dangerous voice:

'So that the young ladies can exchange sweet confidences about their boy friends and their parties and their new clothes. Dearest Mother, what curiously old-fashioned ideas you do have.'

My mother went first very red and then very pale and my father looked at her angrily and after that it wasn't difficult to persuade them that the best place for Janet would be the little room in front. I felt more and more uneasy about the whole business, but it was some comfort that Janet would be as far as possible away from Caroline, whose room was near the kitchen and bathroom at the back of the flat.

I only wished she would retreat there while we were waiting for them to bring Janet back. We were sitting in the waiting-room, just inside the front door, where the television is and where we sit when there are no patients expected. I was feeling intolerably restless and apprehensive and had been messing about switching from one television station to another and turning the sound up and down, hardly aware of what I was doing.

'Is it too much to ask that we should stick to one programme?' asked Caroline.

'Sorry,' I said and turned the set off completely.

'As a matter of fact I was beginning to be interested in that whodunnit,' said Caroline.

'Oh hell. I'm sorry. I'll switch on again.' I jumped up from the chair into which I had flung myself but she reached out an arm to stop me.

'There's not much point now. We've obviously missed

the vital evidence. It looked as if it was going to be quite an original form of murder – working on the old woman's horror of cancer until she was driven to suicide through the conviction that she had it. At least that's how I would guess the plot was working out. What do you think, Richard?'

'What? Oh, the play. I'm sorry. I don't know. I wasn't really taking it in.'

Caroline is very fond of crime stories. So am I. I can never find her enough good ones to satisfy her insatiable appetite and we are sometimes driven to amuse ourselves by concocting ingenious plots of our own. But at the moment I had other things on my mind.

'There they are.' I jumped up again. But the car I had heard didn't stop outside our block. I sat down once more.

'I do wish you'd try and control youself, Dickie dear,' said Caroline. 'We are not expecting a V.I.P. We are awaiting the arrival of our little cousin Janet whom I was always deputed to be kind to and whose existence you were scarcely willing to acknowledge in the days when we were all dumped into the garden at Finchley and told to play together. Silly little snivelling brat,' she concluded with sudden venom.

'She was rather.' I had to admit this. 'But she's changed a lot since then.'

'How do you know? She's never been here to Albany Mansions. Ah yes, of course. You went to see them when you were up in York last year, didn't you?'

'You know perfectly well I did. Don't pretend you've forgotten. You wanted to know all about it when I got home.'

I was standing over Caroline now. I didn't want to say outright that she was jolly well going to be friendly to Janet or else, but I wanted to convey to her that if she was going to be bitchy, then I should take a dim view of it. If only she had shown me that she was anxious and nervous too then I could have been sympathetic and tried to help her, but she had taken up this aloof and hostile attitude and there was no breaking through it. The only thing was to frighten her into behaving decently.

'I do wish you'd sit down and stay sitting,' she said plaintively. 'I'm sure you're still growing taller. It makes one nervous, having a couple of giants in the home.'

I did as she asked. Caroline would be tall too; Caroline would in fact be very elegant and striking if she had legs that would carry her.

'I wish they'd come,' I said. 'I'm dreading this first mealtime.'

'Not as much as she is, I expect,' said Caroline, and I took some hope from the rather more human tone of her voice.

I challenged her to a quick game of Scrabble. We had become superficially absorbed in it when at last the key turned in the lock.

2

JANET PACKINGTON at seventeen was a very different creature from the unhappy little girl whom Caroline and I had bullied into playing games that were too old for her. I had been very agreeably surprised when, in accordance with a promise made to Mother, I had gone to see the family when I was up north the previous summer. Her father was a primary schoolteacher, contented and unambitious, and her mother, my mother's sister, was equally unassuming. They had no other children and they lived in a suburban semi, cheap and neat and glossy, with a dachshund and a canary. They were a devoted trio.

I had felt instantly at ease. No one tried to be clever and we had a North Country high tea and then Janet and I took the dog for a walk. She was taking a secretarial course at the local Tech. and didn't find it necessary to apologise for the fact. She liked children but hadn't had good enough exam results to train to teach, and she was hoping to find a job as a school secretary. She had short fair hair and big grey eyes and when you talked to her she listened carefully, with her mouth very slightly open, ready to break into an encouraging smile or a little droop of sympathy the moment either was required. She asked questions about Caroline and, when I told her, her mouth drooped and she blinked her eyes and then turned her face away. I was very sorry to say good-bye. My home seemed darker than ever when I got back next day.

Two months later came the news that the parents had both been killed in a crash at a crossroads and Janet lay seriously injured in an intensive care unit. My mother rushed up to York to see her and repeated the visit several times during the following weeks. She would never let me accompany her, though. We gathered that although there was plenty of sympathy of the flowers and fruit and visiting sort, finding a suitable home for Janet was going to be a real problem. It was my mother's constant dripping worry about it that led Dad to make the suggestion, and although I became convinced later on that they both had private misgivings about it, once the offer had been made to Janet it was too late to withdraw. The poor kid had jumped at it, naturally enough. Her whole world had fallen to pieces; how could she possibly, in her weak state of convalescence, resist the offer of a home where she would surely receive comfort and sympathy and where she could learn to face each day and build her life again?

But she knew that ours would be a very different sort of household from her own little nest and she must have had qualms too. My first thought when they came into the flat was that she looked completely exhausted. There was no external sign of her injuries but her skin seemed stretched and transparent and her eyes cloudy. My mother had an arm round her and was talking even more quickly and nervously than usual.

'We do so hope you'll be comfortable, darling, it's a bit noisy in front with all the traffic and if you find it too much for you we can easily move you to another room, but I'm afraid we haven't got much of an outlook anywhere in this flat – except in the bathroom where you look right down on the canal —'

The girl didn't seem to hear; she stared straight ahead and moved forward like a sleepwalker. I was standing in the shadow of the hall by the waiting-room door and she hadn't yet noticed me. My father dumped her bags on the floor.

'Where's Caroline?' he asked, and his voice too sounded strained.

'Just coming to join the reception committee.' The wheel of Caroline's chair brushed my ankle as she edged past me through the waiting-room door. 'Hullo, Janet,' she went on brightly. 'It must be six years, mustn't it? We were both very different then.'

She pulled the chair nearer, tilted her head to one side and smiled up at the fair girl but didn't stretch out her hand. Janet took an uncertain step forward and her lips parted in the way I remembered.

'Yes. Six years and two months. When you were living in Finchley.'

Her voice was very faint. She looked as if she was on the point of collapse. I think her whole vision and consciousness must have been temporarily limited to the sight of Caroline's upturned face and self-mocking smile and I don't think she had yet realised that I was there.

'That's right,' cried my mother. 'You remember the apple tree, Janet – they were always trying to drag you up it, my two wicked children —'

She broke off in confusion. My father cleared his throat. Caroline continued to smile. It was a nightmarish moment and I made my first big mistake. My limbs moved of their own accord. I took two long steps forward and picked Janet up and hugged her.

'Hullo, Jan.' I let her down. 'Come on, Mother. She's tired out. Let's get her to bed.'

'Of course, of course.'

My mother burst into feverish activity.

My father said: 'Well, I'll leave you people to it. See you later, Janet, if you feel like sitting up to a meal, though I think you'd be wise to rest now.' He retreated

A MIND TO MURDER

into the consulting-room with evident relief. I picked up
Janet's suitcases.

'Some hot soup, perhaps,' said my mother, fluttering
alongside. 'Or perhaps scrambled egg. Dad's right. I
think you'd better have your supper in bed – I'll bring
you something on a tray —'

'Please, Aunt Phyl. Please I don't want to be a nuisance.
I'm all right. Honestly I am.'

The poor kid could scarcely talk. My mother continued
to fuss. I got her by the shoulders and turned her round
and steered her out of Janet's room. 'What we want is
tea,' I said. 'I do, anyway, and I don't suppose Janet
would say no.'

She went at last, protesting that she would come and
help Janet unpack in a minute. I shut the door behind her
and turned to Janet who was standing miserably in the
middle of the room.

'Quick. Sit down and unwind. She'll be ten minutes at
least. Long enough for some yoga exercises. Do you know
that if you are self-controlled enough you are supposed
to be able to relax so completely within the space of
thirty seconds that it can top you up with energy for the
next twelve hours?'

I went on talking nonsense. Janet lay back against the
divan cushions and smiled faintly. When I paused for
breath she pulled herself upright and looked at me
frowning.

'Caroline,' she began.

I interrupted at once. 'Caroline is all right. She's been
very nervous at the thought of meeting you. She always
is when it's a question of seeing people she hasn't seen
since before her illness. It's perfectly understandable.
She'll be quite all right now. You'll soon get used to
her.'

I spoke with far more conviction than I felt. I had no idea where Caroline was at the moment, but I had no doubt whatever that she was chewing over the way I had stepped forward and kissed Janet and that I could tell her till I was blue in the face that it was like greeting another sister and she would never believe me.

So we got off on the wrong foot from the very start, although I don't suppose it would have made all that difference if I had simply shaken hands formally at that first meeting and either ignored Janet completely thereafter or treated her with cool politeness. Caroline would only have twisted it round and suspected me of hiding my feelings. There was absolutely nothing whatever that either I, or Dad, or Mother, or indeed Janet herself could do that would prevent Caroline from burning herself up inside with jealousy. I think we all realised that, except perhaps Janet herself, at that first meal together.

I managed to protect Janet from Mother's ministrations for long enough to give her a chance to recover a little from her journey and she insisted on joining us in the dining-room for the cold supper we have on Sunday evenings. It was a hideous sort of meal, dominated by the fear that Caroline was going to say something intolerably embarrassing. But she didn't, not on that occasion, and we got through the first week more or less intact. I spent more time than usual with Caroline, and arranged it so that she spent longer in the library at college than usual, waiting for me to collect her and drive her home. Of course she knew perfectly well what I was up to, but I don't think Janet did, and I had the impression that she was rather relieved to find that she wouldn't be seeing much of her cousins because they were so occupied with their studies and their college acquaintances. She began to look a little less exhausted and seemed quite content to chat to Mrs Dring and help her wash up and go for little errands for Mother.

She showed signs of increased nervousness when my father was present, but he made a great effort to be gentle with her and gave her as much outward affection as he is capable of giving anybody. He was very conscious of the fact that she would find us a more intellectual household than she had been used to and he took trouble to explain things to her if a conversation looked like going beyond her grasp. It was well-intentioned but there again I'm not sure that it was altogether wise. Prophets are without honour in their own country and education experts are blind to the problems of their own children, so I suppose it is inevitable that very successful psychiatrists should be incapable of reading people's feelings at their own dinner-table.

'Daddy dear,' said Caroline one evening about ten days after Janet's arrival when my father had been somewhat laboriously expanding on the theory of sublimation of sexual drives, 'Daddy dear, Janet isn't a complete nitwit, you know.'

She shook her head slowly at my father and then winked at Janet, who looked somewhat bewildered and I could only hope that she couldn't read in Caroline's wink all that I could see in it of contempt and dislike. Mother made it worse.

'Never mind, darling,' she said to Janet. 'We can't all be clever and it doesn't make any difference when it comes to finding a good husband. I found one all right and he certainly didn't marry me for my brains.'

Dad gave a little groan and Caroline burst out laughing. 'My honoured parents,' she exclaimed, 'what a positively

Jane Austen conversation! Would you believe it, in this day and age!'

Janet still looked bewildered and I felt very angry with Caroline, although in all fairness she had done nothing openly wrong. Like a fool I had to stick my oar in.

'Oh, I dunno,' I said. 'Most people I know aren't at all keen on having intellectual wives.'

'Is that so?' Caroline cocked her head on one side and looked at me with an air of interested enquiry. 'And what about Mr Duncan Junior? What are his own views in this respect? Is he on the look-out for a gorgeous dumb blonde to match himself?'

I exploded. I do sometimes and am always ashamed of it afterwards. 'Shut up, you bitch!' I yelled. 'I don't want to marry – I only want some *life*!'

This is what Caroline does to you: she sticks a pin in a sensitive spot and it all comes surging out in a flood. It must have been obvious to everyone – my longing to cut loose from this beastly home and choose my own company, my regrets at having turned down that university place I was offered in Scotland in order to stay at home and help. 'God knows I've not had much up till now,' I went on furiously.

I heard my father draw in his breath in pain and my mother give a little sob. Janet's mouth was drooping at the corners and even Caroline stared at me with something like alarm. I could have gone on for hours, flaying them all. It seemed to be coursing through my veins instead of blood, this great stream of anger and resentment. I can't help how I was born, I can't help what I look like, I can't help not being brilliantly clever, I can't help it that my sister is crippled.

Clinging to me, all of them, draining my life away. It'll never be any different. I try to pretend it will but it won't. It's only a daydream that I'll ever be free. It'll follow me always – at home or away. You've got good straight limbs, you're strong and you're healthy, you're stupid and insensitive so you can stand up to anything; you've got to be made to feel guilty always, you've got to be made to pay, pay, pay. Years and years of it, all my life maybe. Wherever I go, whatever I do. All my life ahead and I'm barely twenty-one.

Of course I didn't utter a word of it. I made some sort of apology and sat down again.

'Dear Richard,' said my mother with another sob. 'I really don't know what we'd have done without him, Janet.'

Janet raised her eyes and looked at me with sympathy and Caroline noticed it.

'Well, Daddy,' she said brightly, 'whatever we think of Richard's romantic prospects, at least there is one person's here about which we need have no worry. I don't think you need trouble to explain anything about sex instincts to Janet. I have no doubt she will make up by skill in practice for any lack of comprehension of theory.'

Neither Janet nor my mother fully grasped her point for a moment or two but her very manner of speaking was so offensive that they both flushed. My father very deliberately wiped his mouth with his napkin before speaking.

'Now that's enough, please, Caroline.' It is very rarely indeed that he addresses her in this tone. Usually he will lean over backwards not to reproach her. 'Janet isn't used to the uninhibited manner in which you and Richard have always been encouraged to go on.'

Uninhibited! Christ Almighty! What did he think I was doing now? Choking back everything I was thinking and feeling in me, like a dog swallowing its own vomit.

Mother got us through the rest of the meal by being so very tiresome that she drew everybody's irritation upon herself – deliberately, I am sure, though no doubt she would deny this if challenged with it. The moment I could decently get away I did so. I felt that I ought to have stayed back to reassure Janet, but for the moment I couldn't stand any more. It came pouring through me again the moment I got outside the flat. I never knew I could feel as bad as this. Taking refuge with Lesley or one of the others wasn't going to be any use at all. I began to walk without having the least idea where I was going and went on walking the streets for an hour, stamping it out of my system and trying to exhaust myself.

Eventually I began to feel, if not refreshed, at least a little calmer, and I made my way more slowly homewards. Just before I got back I passed by the little garden where Caroline goes to sit. Of course she wasn't there. It was dark and deserted and the ground was still wet from recently thawed snow. But I paused for a moment at the spot where I believe she normally parks her chair and the thought hit me afresh, hard, relentless and sickening: this is Caroline's freedom, this is the limit of her life.

If I could race around North London and still feel little release from the tide of bitterness and anger that was overwhelming me, what must it be like for Caroline, whose life was one long struggle against far stronger tides, who had hopelessness and physical pain and fear and hellish jealousy to contend with too? The miracle was that she had such amazing self-control, that she didn't collapse more often into those fits of hysterical crying and screaming that shattered us all from time to time. Perhaps, ghastly as such attacks were, it would have been better for us all if she had done so. Perhaps the greatest mistake my father made was that he was constantly boosting her up, praising her intellect and her capacity for adjustment, giving her every possible opportunity to come into contact with people who would stimulate and interest her mind, but no chance at all to be a sick, unhappy child.

I can see his point and his motives were good, no doubt. It's presumptuous of me even to suspect that he might have been influenced by his own pride in Caroline's abilities. But if it had been one of his patients in such a situation and not his own daughter, I can't help feeling that he would have behaved rather differently.

In contrast, his rather ordinary little niece was in quite a different category, more like that of a patient. It was perfectly natural that she should be suffering from shock and grief, and that allowance should be made for this. I am sure it was my father's attitude, as well as the suspicion that I might fall in love with Janet, that led to Caroline's subtle but ever-increasing persecution of Janet.

Caroline had three main ways of getting at her. First of all by using words that Janet didn't know and talking about things that Janet couldn't be expected to understand. Secondly, by harping on Janet's physical attractions. Ostensibly she was simply admiring Janet's clothes or hair-style or make-up, but it was done in an unpleasant and suggestive way – a sort of verbal leering. She was careful not to do this when my parents were present, but she sometimes made such remarks in front of me and I suspect that a great deal of it went on when she and Janet were alone together. Janet took it quite calmly and made no attempt to retaliate and it was only the third method that ever reduced her to showing outward signs of distress.

This involved steering the conversation round to subjects that Janet was obviously anxious to avoid. The first assault was not very subtle. It was inevitable, I suppose, that reference should be made some time or other to the accident that had killed Janet's parents. I believe it was Janet herself who mentioned it first, probably feeling that she ought to force herself to talk of it naturally. She said something about the efficiency of the police and the ambulances, and my parents and I asked a few questions. After a few moments she began to look very pale and tense and we were just about to change the subject when Caroline chipped in:

'Were you conscious, all that time you were trapped in the back of the car and couldn't get out? Do you remember it?'

'I don't really think —', murmured my mother, but Janet interrupted her.

'They said I wasn't unconscious but I don't remember it at all. I had concussion.' Her voice was still under control but one could see that she was beginning to tremble.

'I only wondered,' continued Caroline in the impersonal tones of purely scientific enquiry and staring up at the ceiling in a reflective manner, 'because I imagine it must be rather like being paralysed – to be shut up in the remains of a little metal box and not able to move. I do know just how it must have felt – being trapped – shut in. Oh, I'm so sorry.' She broke off and looked at Janet. 'I'm terribly sorry. Of course you don't want to talk about it. How very stupid of me.'

Janet was shaking uncontrollably. She tried to lift her glass to take a drink of water but only succeeded in splashing some on the table and she put the glass down again without drinking. She gave a little gasp and seemed to be making a tremendous effort to control herself. My mother got up and put an arm round her and persuaded her to leave the room.

'I'll bring her a sedative,' said my father, and I heard him mutter something that sounded like 'residual shock' as he too got up to go. At the door he paused and turned round. 'Better not mention this again to Janet. She may need some help in dealing with the after-effects of shock but family mealtimes are not the right place.'

He had addressed himself as much to me as to Caroline. I felt sure that Caroline's remarks had been cruelly experimental, if nothing worse, but there was no means of proving this, since we were all partly to blame. She never mentioned the accident again in my presence, nor did she speak of accidents in general, but a few days later Janet happened to remark, when she and Caroline and I were discussing likes and dislikes in the animal world, that she couldn't cope with spiders, and after that it was surprising how spiders seemed to keep cropping up in our conversations.

I don't usually take such detailed notice of what people are saying, but I am particularly sensitive in this regard because this is a nasty habit of Caroline's that I have suffered from myself. I'm pretty free from phobias and suchlike on the whole, thank heaven, but I've always had rather a horror at the thought of losing a limb in an accident. Nobody knows this except Caroline and of course she used to taunt me with it when we were kids and I used to rub in her weaknesses – mice and being alone in the dark. But after her illness it turned into something rather more than normal children's crudity, and the sort of thing she would do was to get hold of one of Dad's textbooks on the history of surgery, for instance, pretend she'd found something funny, and then suddenly

33

thrust in front of my eyes some ghastly illustration of a medieval amputation and start laughing.

It doesn't sound very dreadful in itself, but as is always the case with Caroline, it is the *way* she does and says things that is so unpleasant because one is aware of all the vicious thoughts going on in her mind the while.

It is astonishing that my father can ignore this so completely, considering that it is part of his job to understand people's sadistic tendencies, but after all, even psychiatrists are human, and Caroline was once the joy and pride of his life, and now it hurts him all the time and he can't get over it either.

3

JANET had been with us for several weeks and, whatever the state of her nerves, was obviously physically much stronger, when the question of her doing a job arose. She herself made the first suggestion, 'because she couldn't expect to stay here for ever and it was time she began to make a move towards earning her own living.'

I encouraged her to speak to my father. 'I think he's got something in mind,' I added.

'Oh.' She didn't sound altogether pleased. 'Oh well. I don't suppose it matters. I'd rather have got a job of my own accord, though.'

'I can understand that, but I wish you'd let him fix it up for you. It'll give him pleasure. He doesn't get all that satisfaction from his family, poor old Dad.'

'Oh Richard! He does from *you*!'

'Not really. I'm a constant irritant – a reminder of what might have been.'

'Well I don't know what else he could have expected,' she cried warmly. We were sitting together in the waiting-room. Dad was out at a meeting that evening and Mother was helping Caroline to bath. 'I think you're a wonderful son – I think you're absolutely unselfish and kind and steady and thoughtful and loyal, I think you're —'

'Stop, stop!' I yelled, clapping my hands over my ears. 'I can't keep my head on. It's bursting! It's cracking at the seams!'

She laughed and came and sat beside me on the sofa and put her hands over mine and pulled them down. 'It's all right. You can come out now. The compliments session is over.'

'Thank God for that.' I held her hands for a moment and then let them go. I had got to be very, very careful. 'Do you find us very awful, Janet? Do you find it very difficult, living here?'

She considered the questions before replying. 'I don't find *you* awful, but I'm not allowed to talk about that. I find Uncle Andrew a bit alarming, but not so much now that I'm getting used to him, and I really love Aunt Phyllis even if she does ask me again every morning whether I wouldn't try some porridge just to build up my strength.'

'So it's simply Caroline, of course.'

'Why does she dislike me so, Richard? No, please don't pretend. Please. It's much more help if you don't pretend.'

She was sitting perched on the edge of the sofa, her hands clasped on her knees, like a little girl. I leaned across, put an arm under her legs and held them outstretched for a moment. She fell back against the sofa cushions but didn't protest. We both looked down at her nice shapely legs.

'That's why she dislikes you,' I said, letting them drop and sitting upright again.

'But what can I do about it?'

'There's nothing you can do, I'm afraid. I'm in the same boat, you know. Only much worse. You're only a cousin, a temporary interlude. You'll take flight sooner or later. You've not got the same parents, the same memories, the same childhood.'

I didn't want to harp on my own problem but it seemed the only way to make light of hers. 'Honestly I think the only thing you can do is to keep out of her way as much as possible,' I added.

36

'If only I could do something for her —'

'You can't. There's nothing you can do.'

'If she only knew! I – I'm not exactly happy myself, Richard.'

'Good Lord, how on earth should you be? I expect it'll be months before you really begin to see a future. But it's no good appealing to Caroline's sense of pity. I wouldn't say that she is totally wrapped up in her own sufferings and blind to other people, because in fact she is very much aware of other people, but I don't think she'll ever be able to bring herself to offer real sympathy. It's shrivelled up inside her. She hasn't any pity. She hasn't even any pity for herself.'

'No,' said Janet softly. 'She's no pity for herself. That's the worst of all, the way she hits out at herself.'

We were silent for a few minutes, while I thought how enormously comforting it was to be able to talk about Caroline to a sympathetic and understanding person. I don't say much about her to Lesley or any of the others at college, partly because it would be disloyal and partly because I don't want to bore them.

Comforting, but also very dangerous. I was very conscious of Janet sitting only a few inches away on the sofa and I was trying to think of something to say that would ease things off a bit, but not too abruptly, and put a little distance between us, when I surprised myself with the remark that actually came out.

'How far can you walk?'

'Now, do you mean? Or before the accident?'

'Now.'

'Not much more than two or three miles, I should think. I still seem to get tired very easily.'

'Not like our trek with old Sammy! I'm sorry we haven't a dog to take out, but we can take the car up to

37

the Heath and then potter about. Tomorrow afternoon I'm free. Caroline's got a maths seminar. We'll drop her at college and then go on. You're not getting out of the flat enough. You need some fresh air and a change now and then if you're going to be well enough to start work.'

I told myself all the time I was talking that I was being an idiot, but all the same I was disappointed by her response.

'No thanks, Richard. I don't think I want to come anywhere with you, not even for a little stroll. I don't think it's a good idea.'

'I won't take you far. You can come back as soon as you feel tired.'

'It's not that.'

'What is it, then?' I turned and looked closely at her. She flushed.

'I can't explain exactly. I suppose – I suppose it's because I feel I'm in mourning. I mean that walk we had together – it wasn't long after that that Mum and Dad —'

I twisted her face round towards me. 'Now who's doing the pretending? It's because of Caroline, isn't it?'

She went pinker than ever but didn't deny it. 'Don't you think it's for the best?'

'What's for the best? That you deny yourself a piddling little pleasure because you think it might upset Caroline? What the hell d'you think *my* life would be like if I behaved like that all the time?'

'Please, Richard. Please let me go.'

I had to do so.

'It's not quite like that,' she said, rubbing away at her neck where I had touched it, although I knew I couldn't possibly have hurt her at all. 'It's really for my sake more than hers. I'm an awful coward. I'm terribly feeble. So long as I'm living here I know I couldn't really enjoy anything if I knew it was something that Caroline isn't able to do herself.'

I got up and began to move about the room. 'Now this really is plain crazy. I never heard such a daft idea. To what limits do you propose to carry this vow of abstinence? Does it permit you to go to the hairdressers? To go shopping? To go and wallow in a hot bath?'

She looked at me steadily. 'Don't sneer at me, Richard. It's not fair. It's not like you.'

'Isn't it indeed? You don't know what is or isn't like me. You don't know anything about me at all, do you?'

'I think I do. You look very like your father just now.'

'Damn you.' For some reason this got right under my skin. 'Well, I think you're a bloody fool. You'll never be able to keep it up and it won't help Caroline at all.'

'I'm not thinking of Caroline. I'm thinking of me.'

'I still think you're a fool. I won't have it, Janet. You can stop this nonsense right away.'

'And you can stop shouting at me.'

She got to her feet and we glared at each other. Her lips twitched very slightly but I was feeling much too irritated to interpret it as amusement. 'You're an obstinate, pig-headed little girl,' I said.

'And you're nothing but a bully,' she retorted. 'I take back all I was saying earlier. I'm very sorry for Caroline, having such a brother.'

She dodged past me and made for the door. I was left with my fingers grasping at air, cursing myself and wondering how on earth I was going to refrain from grabbing her next time we were alone for a while together.

I wasn't put to the test for some time, however, since Janet scarcely spoke to me during the next few days,

which might have been due to caution or might have been
a piece of tactical flirtation. I hoped that Caroline hadn't
noticed anything, but one can never be quite sure what
Caroline has or hasn't noticed. And one can also never
be quite sure what she has overheard. We have thick
fitted carpets throughout the flat and her chair moves very
smoothly and silently. Once or twice when I've come
out of a room where I'd been talking to somebody and
the door had been left slightly ajar, I have had the distinct
impression that Caroline had been in the corridor outside
and had got herself out of sight when she realised someone was leaving the room. I've never actually caught her,
and I wouldn't want to hurt her by accusing her of
eavesdropping, and in any case she would only make the
excuse that she was having trouble with her chair or
needed help in doing something.

I didn't see how she could possibly have overheard
Janet and me talking in the waiting-room that evening,
however, because when I came out and went along to the
kitchen at the back of the flat to satisfy a sudden urgent
hunger, there were Mother and Caroline just coming out
of the bathroom next to it. Caroline has a contraption
which enables her to bath, but she still needs Mother's
help and she couldn't possibly have got into her chair and
raced to the front of the flat to listen to me and Janet
talking and then back again to the bathroom without
Mother knowing. All the same, she said something that
made me feel uneasy.

'Hullo, Richard. Whither away so fast? I thought you
and Janet were watching television. Is it over? Or have
you quarrelled?'

I must have shown in my manner that I was feeling
somewhat aggravated. Caroline would guess the rest. For
all I knew she might well believe that I'd already been

making love to Janet. In which case, I thought angrily, I might just as well have the pleasure of justifying her suspicions. So considering the mood I was in, it was probably just as well that Janet was particularly careful during those next few days though her resolution to take part in nothing that Caroline couldn't share was not put to the test either since the occasion didn't arise.

She duly mentioned to my father that she would like to start work and he took her along to the hospital with him one morning to be introduced to Matron. Naturally it all had to be discussed over the dinner-table that evening. That's the worst of families.

'When do you start, Janet?' asked Caroline amiably enough.

'Next Monday. I'm to work mornings only for a week alongside the girl who is leaving and then full-time on my own the week after.'

Janet was paler than usual but quite composed. None of us had the least inkling then that she was scared stiff of the job, although my mother did start her usual line about Janet not overdoing things.

'Oh, for heavens' sake don't fuss so, Mummy!' Caroline, oddly enough, was the one to come to the rescue. 'You can't keep Janet trailing round after you and Mrs Dring any longer. Of course she wants to get out of the flat and do a proper job.'

If anyone else had said this it would have been taken at its face value as a sympathetic and encouraging remark. But spoken by Caroline one's first thought was inevitably that she, Caroline, would never be able to get out and do a proper job and she wanted to remind us all of this. Poor Caroline! Was it her fault or ours that she was always taken in this way? Janet, of course, was super-sensitive about it.

'I'll be all right, Aunt Phyl. Honestly. It's high time I was earning some money. I've got to start earning my living.'

I think she was laying undue stress on the financial factor out of sheer embarrassment, out of that feeling that Caroline always arouses in you, that you have to prove you have difficulties and problems too.

'Well, my dear, you know you haven't to worry about that just yet,' said my mother. 'You've got that insurance money of your father's, and you'll have the balance of the money from the sale of the house – if ever those wretched solicitors get the business done – and in any case you know you can always depend on us. We only want to help you, don't we, Andrew?'

'Of course. But it will be better if Janet doesn't dip into her capital. She'll be needing it when she marries and starts her own home.'

A perfectly sensible and harmless remark of my father's. But nothing is harmless when there are under-currents of feeling such as there are in my family. It set Caroline off, of course.

'In any case,' she said in the tone of voice that I dread to hear, 'as Daddy is going to have to provide for a crippled daughter for life it won't be much of an extra burden to fork out for a little while for an orphaned niece.' She laughed.

One can envisage a hopelessly sick person saying this sort of thing without arousing any emotion except sympathy and goodwill all round. But not Caroline. She intends it to hurt and shock and it does.

'That's what *you* think,' said my father in a falsely hearty voice. 'You're going to earn your living too, my girl. Don't you go thinking you're getting out of that.'

'I thought it was all arranged,' broke in my mother.

'Isn't Caroline going to do computer programming or something? I thought she was doing that special course in her work for her degree —'

My poor mother floundered on wretchedly.

'No, no, you've got it all wrong as usual,' snapped my father, and he began to explain, as if to an idiot child, the nature of Caroline's studies. Caroline herself joined in, and Mother muttered distractedly at intervals: 'Of course you're all so clever – so clever.'

I'm very used to this sort of thing and I'm afraid I sometimes take part in it too. But this time there was a clear-sighted observer present at the family ritual. I glanced at Janet and saw surprise and something like distaste in her face and suddenly, to my own great discomfort, I saw us all through her eyes. With a similar flash, the memory of that afternoon I had spent at their home in York returned to me: her father and his tales of naughty boys at school, her mother's infectious chuckle, and above all Janet herself, happy and beloved and at ease, instead of this pale wraith sitting here afraid to say anything but none the less keeping her own standards flying in her mind and reserving her judgement on us all.

I think I must have fallen in love with my cousin – seriously I mean – that evening, so I suppose I was largely responsible for all that followed after.

4

JANET started her job and was so tired when she got home in the evenings that there was no question of trying to make her break her resolution to do nothing that Caroline couldn't do. Even my father expressed some concern about her, while my mother worried non-stop about her being overworked.

Janet had also slipped into the habit of doing little things in the flat – tidying the papers in the waiting-room, giving the flowers fresh water, putting new telephone message pads by the telephone and clean towels and toilet paper in the bathroom – all trivial things in themselves, but the sum total of them made a noticeable difference to the comfort and appearance of the household. Unfortunately this led to a quarrel between my parents, Dad accusing Mother of making Janet do housework, and my mother retorting that she had been forced into a job she wasn't fit for. All this took place at half past nine in the evening in the waiting-room. Janet had gone to bed very early and I had no idea where Caroline was. It ended with both my parents appealing to me, speaking alternately:

'What do you think, Richard?'

'You're more in her confidence than anyone else.'

'Has she mentioned anything to you?'

It shook me rather to realise that I was assumed to be so close to Janet and after a moment's reflection I could only say that I thought Janet liked going to work at the hospital and would be sorry to give it up. Usually in an argument I find myself tending to side with my mother, but I had a special reason for taking the opposite view now. I had begun to be quite alarmed by the expression that I sometimes caught on Caroline's face when she looked at Janet. It was the way she occasionally looked at me, as if she was longing for fate to deal me a blow such as the one she had received herself; full of hatred, almost evil. I don't think my parents ever noticed it, or if they did they managed to suppress their awareness, and I don't think Janet had noticed – at any rate I prayed that she hadn't. But I couldn't help feeling that the more Janet was out of the flat the better it would be for her, and it was surely better for her to be overworked at the hospital than to be subjected to Caroline's venom at home, particularly as we had reached the Easter vacation and Caroline was not even out at lectures and classes.

My mother looked at me reproachfully and my father said: 'The boy's right, Phyllis, and if you'd only stop asking her to do all these errands for you she wouldn't get so tired.'

'I don't ask her!' cried my mother. 'She does things of her own accord. She's a thoroughly considerate, well-brought-up girl —'

'There's no earthly need for her to be mending the bed linen,' interrupted my father.

'She says she likes sewing. Why shouldn't she? Mrs Dring's got more than enough to do as it is. I suppose you think I'm not pulling my weight but how I can possibly be expected to do any more when there's all that I have to do for Caroline —'

'Nobody is suggesting for one moment that you should try to do any more. You always will take everything so personally. But I do think you might let Caroline try and do a bit more for herself. There's no need to make a baby of her.'

'I like that, I like that!' almost screamed my mother.

It is not often that she gets as worked up as this but there is no stopping her when she does. 'Just you try telling that to Caroline! All right, I know you're always telling me not to fuss her and I know she's very good and brave about trying to do things – but it's only the things she wants to do. Just you suggest she should do something she doesn't want to, just you try suggesting she should help mend the linen – that's something she *could* do to help me! – or even mend her own clothes – and see what reaction you get!'

'Hush, Phyllis. Hush, dear. Try and calm yourself.' My father took a step towards her but she flounced away.

'You don't know what my life is like – you've no idea. You've always encouraged Caroline to think that nothing matters but her brains and now she hasn't got anything but her brains and she knows it's not true. She was never taught to be patient and resigned and think of others. Never, never. And it's too late now. It's hopeless. Hopeless.'

My mother began to cry loudly and when my father moved towards her again this time she did not try to push him away. They clung together, mingling their grief. They had forgotten that I was in the room. I think they had probably forgotten my existence. I moved silently past them and out of the room and as I stepped into the hall I had the strong impression that something had just passed down the corridor – it was as if the slight disturbance of the air caused by Caroline rushing along in her wheelchair was still to be felt. If I had instantly taken long strides down the corridor I might have caught her at the door of her room, might even have wrung from her a confession that she had been eavesdropping; might possibly have been able to act as comforter and troubleshooter and so prevent my parents' remarks from adding yet further to her sum total of bitterness and misery.

If there had been no Janet this is probably what I would have done. As it was, I told myself that I must have been mistaken. Caroline was obviously getting on with her reading in her own room. Ours is a solid old building and she couldn't, at the back of the flat, have heard anything of my parents' quarrel.

If anyone had heard, it was more likely to be Janet. I turned left, past the consulting-room door, and stopped outside the door of Janet's room. There was a thread of light underneath. She hadn't gone to sleep yet, then. I knocked softly.

'Who's that?'

It was a very frightened little voice and I couldn't help wondering if she expected it to be Caroline.

'Only me – Richard. Can I come in? I only want to ask you something. I won't stay long.'

'Just a minute.'

There was a scuffling sound and then she came to the door in her dressing-gown, looking very pink and embarrassed. I was puzzled. Janet is quite natural and unaffected and I wouldn't have said she suffered from false modesty. There had to be some other explanation for her confusion than the obvious one that she had just gone to bed. I glanced round the room. Apart from the fact that the divan cover and the bedclothes were drawn back and the pillows puffed up, it looked just as it did at any other time. She'd evidently actually been in bed. I was about to pull the blankets up again and throw the cover over them so as to make it more comfortable to sit on when she became more agitated than ever, pushed me aside, and hastily plumped herself down on the turned-over bedclothes.

47

'What on earth's the matter with you, Jan?' I asked.
'Are you afraid I'm going to rape you or something?'

She shook her head briskly from side to side but did
not budge from her awkward position, perched on top of
the folded-over covers. At that moment it occurred to
me that she was hiding something – literally sitting on
it. I was too curious to be delicate and I simply heaved
her up and dumped her down again on the far end of
the divan. Then I turned back the bedclothes to reveal
a little blue-jacketed book and a larger blue exercise
book.

'What on earth —', I began, picking them up and
staring at them. '"Twenty Lessons in Shorthand".' I
opened the exercise book. Several pages of it were
covered with hieroglyphics. I had to laugh. 'Dearest
Janet! Why this terrible secrecy? I thought at least you'd
got *Fanny Hill* or the *Khama Sutra* concealed under
there.'

She was as red in the face as if she had. She looked at me
pathetically but said nothing.

'But why do you have to hide a textbook on shorthand? What's the dreadful secret? Do tell me, Jan.'

She began to talk at last, hesitantly. 'Because I'm so
ashamed – because I never finished my secretarial course
properly – because I'm not very good at shorthand and
keep making mistakes at work. Matron's very patient
considering and I thought if I could learn it up a bit in the
evenings —'

'So that's what's been worrying you and making you
look so washed out.'

I couldn't help smiling again. When I thought of all
the agonies my parents had been going through and
realised they were due to nothing more desperate than
the fact that Janet felt a bit shaky with her shorthand!

What a descent from the tragic to the absurd! But evidently it was no joke to her.

'I still don't understand,' I said more seriously. 'If you didn't feel up to the job why didn't you say so? Or at any rate why didn't you say that you needed practice with shorthand? We could have helped you. One of us could easily have dictated slowly to you and given you practice.'

Her lip began to quiver and tears came into her eyes. She brushed them aside and jumped to her feet and turned on me suddenly.

'You'd have sneered at me, wouldn't you? All you terribly clever people and silly cousin Janet can't even learn to write shorthand!'

I stared at her speechless. It might have been my mother speaking, but I was shocked and hurt in a way that I never am by Mother.

'I don't think you're being quite fair,' I said at last. 'I would never have sneered at you and neither would my parents. They only want to help you.'

'Caroline would have.'

She was audibly sobbing now.

'Let's leave Caroline out of this, shall we? She's in rather a special category.'

I sat down heavily on the divan and picked up the textbook and began to study it. If I didn't do something quickly to occupy myself I was going to get hold of her and this time it was going to be impossible to let go. 'Lord, how complicated!' I exclaimed. 'It's as bad as chemical formulas when you don't know them, but when you do, it's easy. Or should be.' I turned the pages. 'Oh, I see. You don't go by spelling or actual letters of the alphabet. It's the sound of it that matters.'

I went on reading, taking no notice of her. I think she

moved over to the mirror to check on her face. I picked
up the exercise book and threw it in her direction. 'Here –
get a pencil. Sit down. We'll have a little practice.
Imagine I'm an overweight, expense-account-fed execu-
tive – a tyrannical tycoon —'

I glanced up and saw her smile, and then she picked up
the exercise book and we worked away most conscien-
tiously at shorthand for the next hour. Then I stood up
and yawned.

'Gosh, it's exhausting. Hope I've not kept you up too
late. I'm going to know as much as you do by the time
we've finished at this rate.'

She jumped quickly into bed and pulled the covers up
to her chin. 'Thank you, Richard, thank you, thank —'

Her voice trailed away. The grey eyes looked at me. I
yawned again, stretched, shook myself violently. 'No
objection to learning it myself – come in very useful for
lectures, 'nother session tomorrow. G'night.'

I got myself out of the room. But not in these circumstances, I added to myself; it's too great a strain. And
then I couldn't help smiling to think what the psychiatrists would say. But it's not sex she's needing, it's
shorthand, I added to myself.

Finding opportunities for helping Janet without anyone else knowing presented quite a problem. The only
times I really felt safe were when Caroline was out of the
flat. Unfortunately it was a very cold spring and the
weather was not often suitable for her to take her little
independent outings. Nor did she appear as willing as
usual to go for drives or to theatres and concerts with my
parents. In fact it was very difficult to get her out of the
flat at all and although she always made the excuse that she
was too busy or too tired I didn't believe it for a moment.

Usually I spend part of each vacation with Brian. We went all through school together and although he went straight into an insurance company instead of going to university I still feel happier with him than with any more recent friends. He's a solid, plodding sort of chap but with a nice unexpected vein of humour and he has always got on well with Caroline. It was a loss when his people left our part of the world and went to live in Cardiff and he decided to settle there too. When something was mentioned about my going there I glanced at Janet and saw that she was not only startled but looked positively frightened.

'I don't think I'll go down to Wales this Easter,' I said quickly. 'I've got too much work. It's only six weeks till Finals.'

This was accepted with some surprise but without much comment, except that Caroline wanted to know which girl-friend was responsible for keeping me in London, and she continued to harp on the theme, always with sideways glances at Janet to see how she was taking it.

'As a matter of fact,' I said suddenly, 'I'm asking Brian here.'

This caused further surprise and my mother immediately plunged us into the problem of where he was going to sleep and similar matters. My plan was to enlist Brian's help. I knew he would be willing to come and I was equally sure that once the situation was explained to him, he would take Caroline off my hands for a few hours each day.

I don't think I was quite myself at that period. What with the strain of wanting Janet so desperately and feeling guilty about neglecting Caroline, and worrying that Caroline was being beastly to Janet, and on top of this all the worry about my exams – because I'd no hope of sailing through easily and knew I'd really have to swot at it to get even a tolerable degree – I had got into quite a feverish and unbalanced frame of mind and it was extraordinary that my parents were so totally unaware of it. It took the form of an absolute obsession with the idea of getting Janet to myself for a while and in particular of taking her out for an evening.

Brian came and was a tower of strength. He told me off about behaving rather peculiarly and I told him everything except my own fears of what Caroline was capable of. That seemed to me to be too disloyal, but he quite realised that she was extremely jealous and he did manage, very cleverly, to give me a chance at any rate to have a few hours at Janet's shorthand in peace.

We boobed over the evening out, though.

After vain attempts to get Caroline to go to a play with Brian that she had expressed an interest in but which nobody else wanted to see, I decided at last that it would have to be by a trick. Brian and I would tell Caroline that we were going out together for the evening, but in fact we would immediately part company and arrange to meet some hours later. He would amuse himself as best he could and I would go straight to St Martin's Hospital, collect Janet and convince her that Brian had taken Caroline out and that there was no reason in the world why she herself shouldn't spend the evening with me. The worst bit would be persuading her to phone home to tell Mother that she was going out with one of the girls at the hospital, but I'd no doubt that when it came to the point I'd be able to overcome her scruples. And then of course we'd have to arrive home separately so that Caroline would suspect nothing, but that hurdle could also be taken when the moment arrived.

I really think I must have been a little mad. Brian said I was. He said it was like one of those tiresome gallants in Restoration comedy, devoting enormous thought and effort and strategy towards getting into some woman's bedroom – 'but you're not even aiming at abduction or seduction,' he concluded with disgust. I said I knew I was being idiotic but begged him to bear with me.

It was a terrible evening. First of all I had a hell of a job to persuade Janet to come out with me at all. Then she flatly refused to pretend to my mother that she was with one of the girls and in the end I had to ring Mother myself and explain and swear her to secrecy. She promised not to let on to Caroline, but I felt most uneasy about it and was not at all sure that Caroline wasn't overhearing Mother's end of the conversation. So I was worrying about this all through dinner and all through the film that we went to because Janet said she hadn't got the energy to dance, and she sat there gloomily in the cinema too. When we came out I simply hadn't the face to explain that we'd have to go home separately, and of course I was supposed to be meeting Brian, who as far as Janet knew, was supposed to have been taking Caroline to the theatre.

So in the end I had to confess it all, although I think she had more or less guessed it for herself by then. She was extremely angry and refused to speak to either Brian or myself on the way home. Her lips were clamped together as I had never seen them before. It made me so wretched that I was beyond caring who knew what about anything.

We came into the flat about half past eleven and I wasn't in the least surprised to find that Caroline had not yet gone to bed but was in fact actually coming into the hall at the same moment as we did. She looked at each of us in turn but said nothing and continued to make her way along the corridor. Janet marched straight over to her room and slammed the door behind her. My mother appeared from somewhere and started on a long explanation which I cut short rudely. And just as a little garnish to top it all, my father had to arrive a moment later, having been at a professional conference where he'd had a bitter argument with some of his colleagues about a new kind of treatment and he was obviously in the foulest of tempers.

The only thing to be said for the whole silly business was that it cured me of my obsession. My feeling for Janet was if anything stronger than ever, but I resolved that I would not try to take her out again at least until after my exams were over. I consoled myself with making plans for the future. I would get my degree, take the best paid job I could find, and make a home for her.

I would have liked to tell her about it – in my conceit I took it for granted that she was feeling the same way about me – but she became very unapproachable after that evening and wouldn't even let me help her with her shorthand. Caroline seemed to withdraw into herself more too. Brian went home, and I discovered with horror that the exams were rushing upon me. The sensible thing to do was to concentrate upon my work and not to think about people and their feelings at all for the time being, and this I did my very best to carry out.

5

I SPENT a lot of time in the library and the labs at college and when I was at home I shut myself up in my room. There's one thing to be said for my family. At least one couldn't have a better home from which to take exams. Nobody disturbed me and my mother slaved away more than ever cooking me snacks at odd hours so that I didn't have to come and eat with the others if I didn't want to be interrupted at that moment. My father actually took a little time off from his reading and writing to come and talk over various developments in chemical therapy with me and Caroline hardly mentioned my exams at all, for which I was grateful.

As for Janet, I barely saw her. She went off to work before I got up in the morning – I found it easiest to work at night so I tended to sleep late – and when she got home I was usually still in the library or already closeted in my bedroom. Two or three days before my first paper I managed to catch her alone for a moment and asked her if she was finding the job a bit easier now and she nodded and smiled, looking more like her old self, and assured me that she was racing away with her shorthand.

'I only wish I could help you as much as you helped me,' she added.

'It won't be long now.' I gave an exaggerated sigh. 'I suppose I'll survive. Other people seem to.'

'I dare say you will. You'll do better than your worst fears but not as well as your secret hopes.'

'Janet.' I caught her arm. We were standing just outside the door of her room. 'That sounds terribly sensible. And typical of you.'

She laughed. 'Oh, it's not original. It's what Daddy used to say. Good luck, Richard. If I don't get a chance to say it to you at zero hour I'm saying it now. Good luck.' And she had stood on tiptoe and raised her hands and encircled my face and kissed me and disappeared so quickly that I was scarcely conscious of what she was doing until it was over.

It did me more good than anything, that little conversation. It made me more tolerant of my father's anxious looks and my mother's ignorant reassurances. 'Of course you'll do well. Of course you will.' She said this over and over again during the last few days. It was as if she was talking more to herself than to me.

I was in a terrible panic, but no worse than everyone always is I suppose, when something happened on the Monday evening before I was to sit the first paper that very nearly prevented me from putting in an appearance on the Tuesday morning at all.

I'd walked home from college. It wasn't a pleasant walk, much of it being through great areas of half-finished flyovers and decaying terraces, but it worked off some of the tension and made me think of little else but the welcome contrast of being comfortable at home again. The last half-mile was the worst stretch of all, between acres of disused railway land – old sidings, sheds, platforms – that was scheduled for re-development within the next year or two. It was far too complicated and extensive to police adequately and it was the haunt of tramps and drop-outs of every kind. The hoardings were constantly being broken down and although it was a fairly busy road for motor traffic, one rarely saw any pedestrians there except members of the nomad population. So-called 'decent' citizens avoided walking that way.

I don't think I am any more cowardly than anyone else, but I did find myself glancing around me and taking longer strides as I covered the last half-mile and when I reached the spot where the road crosses the canal in a sort of half-bridge (beyond that the canal goes underground) I leant on the parapet with a sensation of relief. This was the boundary line; on the other side was our own area – ugly but expensive and perfectly respectable. I glanced in the direction of our flats – I couldn't see the back of them from where I stood owing to a slight curve in the waterway – and then down at the dirty water beneath. They were supposed to be cleaning the canal up eventually and making some kind of riverside walk, but that was at the moment something of a dream. Meanwhile it was most unappetising, with the crumbling towpaths on either side, and after a few moments I turned away and walked on.

Another couple of minutes brought me to the gardens where Caroline sits. On other occasions I have walked straight past without looking for her but this evening I had an absurd sentimental impulse to try to recapture my childhood, an idiotic idea that at this crisis in my life my sister would surely be having some kindly feelings towards me. I would see if Caroline was there, and if she was in the right mood, then I would remind her of the times we used to swot over our maths together; when although two years her elder, I was always several moves behind her quicker understanding. Whatever her own unhappiness, in spite of everything I was the human being nearest to her. She surely couldn't refuse to give me her blessing at this moment.

It was a dull, coolish evening for early June and there was scarcely a soul about. I didn't think it very likely that she was there but there was no harm in strolling round to see. In one corner of the gardens there is a group of shrubs, providing cover from the roadway and growing in a half-circle to give shelter from the wind to a couple of seats. I approached this shrubbery from the side, so that I could not actually see the benches and the patch of gravel on which they stood, but when I was a few yards away I noticed what looked like the wheel of Caroline's chair showing beyond the base of a sparsely leaved bush.

I hesitated. There was nobody else in sight. This was her only time of complete privacy and independence. She was quite alone. It was unfair to intrude. I could talk to her later in the evening if she was at all approachable.

And then I heard it. A low muttering sound interspersed with little squeaking noises. My first thought was that she had come to grief, slipped from the chair and hurt herself and been unable to get up. I was going to rush forward and then once more I hesitated. Perhaps she wasn't hurt at all; perhaps this was the way she let off steam, relieved her feelings when she was quite alone. Rather like me singing loudly out of tune when I'm going for a walk by myself. So I took a few cautious steps nearer. More of the chair came into view and part of an arm. The branches hid her head but I had the impression that she was bending over something. I crept forward again, taking great care to make no sound, disgusted with myself for spying but unable to resist the impulse. The strange noises continued. What on earth was she doing?

I manœuvred myself into a position where I gained a better view. She seemed to be totally absorbed; there was no question of her having heard me.

And then suddenly I saw. And it was so horrible that a sort of convulsion came over me and it was all I could do not to cry out. I had found out what Caroline does when she goes and sits in the gardens by herself: she tortures little birds.

She'd got hold of something still alive – a sparrow, I suppose – and as far as I could see she was pulling out feathers, slowly, deliberately, mumbling away all the time. I think she was doing something else to it too but I didn't want to know. I stepped back away from the shrub and very nearly vomited. She must have heard something then because the muttering stopped. I came round the bushes to face her as if I had only just arrived and I stopped short of her chair.

She glanced up at me and I caught a lingering trace of what her face must have looked like a moment before. It was more than enough. She quickly brought herself under control.

'Look, Richard.' She gave me her pathetic little smile and held out the remains of the sparrow. 'Look – isn't it sad. I've just picked it up off the ground here. A cat must have been at it. I don't think it's quite dead yet.'

I snatched the thing from her, tried not to look at it, quickly wrung its neck and flung it into the bushes.

She pretended to shudder. 'Oh Dickie! How can you do it! – so brutal. I don't think I could do it myself. Poor little dicky-bird.'

'Only thing to do when a creature's badly injured like that,' I snapped and I knew even as I said it that I wasn't going to say anything more, that I was going to pretend too. She gave me a very odd look indeed.

'Do you include me within the category of badly damaged creatures who ought to be destroyed?' she asked.

'Oh shut up, Carol. Don't be so silly. Isn't it getting rather cold? Hadn't you better come in?'

'Shut up yourself. Don't do a "Mother" on me.'

She picked up a book that was tucked down in her chair and ostentatiously began to read.

'All right then,' I said and turned away.

It was only a few yards to walk home but I felt so sick and shaken that it was all I could do to get there. I'm not squeamish and have done plenty of dissection at one time or another, but this just turned my stomach. It's one thing to take dead animals to pieces in the course of one's studies but quite another thing to pull to pieces, gloatingly and deliberately, still living creatures. How did she get hold of it, I wondered; perhaps a cat really had begun the job. Perhaps she did something to the cats too. Perhaps even a little child – Christ! I would have to tell someone, have to do something.

I tried to think clearly as I staggered the last few yards. My mother – overburdened already. How could I possibly describe it to her and watch the sickening disgust appear on her face? My father – with Caroline his broken joy. How could I bring myself to give him such a fresh blow? Perhaps I'll sleep on it, I thought, and then: if I sleep at all – it's exams tomorrow. And by the time I had shut the front door of the flat behind me I felt so ill and desperate that I had stopped trying to think at all and only knew that I must find some help quickly.

I got to the door of the consulting-room. I didn't stop to knock, but rushed straight in. Fortunately there was no patient there.

'Dad!' I cried. 'Please help – I feel like – dying!'

I've often felt bitter against my father for assuming I have no problems and that he never need bother about me, but that evening he couldn't have done more. He didn't speak at all, but eased me into a chair and felt my pulse and had a closer look at me, and then he fished out some marvellous pills that had the almost immediate effect of putting things at a distance so that they didn't matter so much any more; and then he sat down and talked for a while very calmly and soothingly about ordeals in general and taking exams in particular, and how having fits of panic beforehand was a good omen for being very much on top of things when it came to the point – no complicated psychological theories, just comforting commonsense like Janet's father would have talked.

When I began to yawn a bit he suggested I should go straight to my room and he promised to keep Mother and everyone else out of the way and to bring me something to eat himself if I wanted it, and also some real knockout sleeping drug, but I wasn't to worry that I wouldn't wake in time because they'd see to that, and I ought not to feel any dopy after-effects but if I did there was a very mild sort of pep pill that was quite harmless and didn't affect your thinking ability but that would get you started.

It all went according to plan. I went out like a light and awoke a different person. My mother brought me some breakfast in bed and my father put his head round the door to say good luck. I didn't see either Janet or Caroline. They had faded right away. It was as if I was eighteen months old again and we were a little family of three. I felt positively cheerful as I banged the front door behind me and at ten o'clock I was sitting staring at blank sheets of paper with not a thought in my head except the problem of whether I was going to remember the essential facts of molecular orbital theory.

I didn't hurry away after the second paper that day but hung about exchanging notes and holding post-mortems with fellow-sufferers, so that by the time I got home they had all had their evening meal and dispersed. This too was in accordance with my father's plan. I did feel a little qualm of conscience when remembering what Caroline had done the evening before, but it all seemed a long time ago and very unreal. Perhaps I had only imagined it.

The more I thought about it, the more likely did this explanation seem. There certainly had been a sparrow, but the strong probability was that it really had been mauled by a cat and she had been doing nothing more than investigate whether it was beyond saving. I had been terribly worked up and apprehensive about my exams. My mind might have created its own horrors. Caroline could be destructive and even venomous in her words and general behaviour; she was quite capable of reading people's private correspondence and making use of information gained, and I wouldn't even put it past her to write poison-pen letters if the occasion arose; but the actual infliction of physical pain on something weaker than herself – no, that wasn't in character, that wasn't subtle enough. I persuaded myself that I had been mistaken, and if my mind reverted to the matter during the days that followed, it was only to deepen in this conviction. But in fact I soon ceased to think about it at all.

One can't be said to be a normal human being at all during the days of doing examinations. Of course there is some visible object that people take to be you and that moves and talks and eats and sleeps outside the lab and the examination hall, but it doesn't seem to be part of yourself and is remote and dreamlike. The only reality is the long room with the lines of grim, hunched figures, and the little dais where the invigilator sits, and the jerking hands of the electric clock above his head.

So the days went by. Three weeks, on and off, had to be got through, and the days interspersed between the written and the practical papers were particularly trying, a sort of no-man's land where one didn't fully belong either to the bustling, careless world outside the long windows, nor to the moving minute-hand world within. My father insisted that I should go away during this gap. I didn't want to go and leave Janet, because although I had hardly spoken to her during the exam days, I felt it must be some reassurance to her to know that I was coming in and out of the flat, but I couldn't think up any excuse that would do for Dad and so I had to go.

I went down to Brian's and he took a few days' leave and we drove and walked and talked and I did a certain amount of revision. I didn't tell him of my plan to marry Janet and when he asked about her I was rather offhand. Usually I pour out everything to Brian and I can't understand why I was reticent about this. I told myself it was because he had been bored by it all enough on his last visit to us, but I don't think that was really the reason. Perhaps I thought he would not be sympathetic; perhaps I was afraid it would be tempting Providence.

I wasn't supposed to be coming home until late on the Sunday evening before the week of practical work began, but by the Saturday afternoon Brian's soothing influence was beginning to wear off and the trials of the days ahead began to weigh heavily on me. The thought of a long Sunday of pottering about was intolerable; I felt I had to get back and at least gain the illusion that I was preparing myself. So I returned to London very late on the Saturday evening without telling anyone I was arriving since I knew Dad would disapprove, and hoping to creep in without anyone knowing.

The flat was very quiet and felt more oppressive than ever. There was no light burning. I turned the key very carefully, slid my suitcase along the carpet and crept across the hall. I would use the washroom in front and not go to the back of the flat at all. But when I was closing the door behind me, I was exceedingly startled to hear a voice call sharply: 'Who's that?'

'Good Lord!' I cried. 'Janet!'

I don't know why I was so surprised. It would have been odd if she had heard nothing. Perhaps my examination nerves were affecting me more than I had realised. For one moment I had actually forgotten that she was sleeping next door to the washroom; I had really believed there to be no one in the front of the flat.

She was very near to me in the darkness. I could hear her breathing, rather quickly and unevenly. I could see her in my mind's eye. I kept still with an effort.

'Ssh,' I whispered, 'I don't want any of them to know I'm here.'

'I won't tell them,' she whispered back, and then added with a little catch in the voice that was an invitation in itself, 'but I'm so glad you are.'

I got myself away somehow without touching her, felt my way into the waiting-room, curled up on the sofa, clung to the cushions and suffered hours of very wretched wakefulness, cursing everybody and everything. Damn the girl; why did she have to come at one like that? Didn't she *know* what it did to one? Hadn't I got enough to worry about at the moment without having to go into agonies of self-restraint? Could she really be so very young and simple?

For a while I raged at her in my mind. And then a small voice of reason intervened: hadn't she behaved perfectly naturally? She had heard someone moving outside her door late at night and had come out to see what was happening. For all she knew I might have been a burglar. She had done nothing wrong. I alone was to blame. And then the voice of reason went on: anyway, you're going to marry her, so why wait, what does it matter? I couldn't answer this; I only knew that it did matter, terribly. Janet wasn't like the others; Janet was different.

And so the night passed away.

There was a certain amount of surprise the following morning, but no reproaches, when my parents discovered me. Caroline was sleeping late and didn't appear at breakfast, and I thought my parents both seemed tired and depressed. Janet pretended she hadn't known I was back, but she seemed low in spirits too, and when Mother asked me what I was going to do that day, I thought Janet looked at me wistfully.

'I'll probably go and look up some of my fellow victims,' I said in a noncommittal way and I thought I saw Janet look disappointed.

But look darling, I found myself arguing with her in my mind; it's no good. If I stay in I'll only want to take you back to bed and it's not practicable, apart from everything else. And if I take you out I'm going to be a miserable sort of companion, quite apart from Caroline. We'll just have to stick it out; it's not much longer. As soon as exams are over we'll get engaged and do as we like – as *you* like rather. I tried to tell her this by the way I looked at her; I couldn't trust myself to talk about it.

'Only another week, Jan. Then we're really going to celebrate, you and I.' This was all I dared say.

It was a relief to get away from home. I went off without having seen Caroline, for which I wasn't sorry, and without any clear idea of where I was going. But as usual in such circumstances my feet turned in the direction of the road where Lesley lived, only twenty minutes' walk away. She shared the basement of an old terrace house with another girl from college, who opened the door before I had rung the bell and said she was just going out.

'It's all yours,' she added, waving back at me from half-way up the area steps.

I took this to mean that Lesley was not otherwise engaged and gave a great sigh of relief. The hours until next morning's practical, which had seemed a short while ago to stretch to infinity, suddenly telescoped into a manageable space of time. I shut the front door behind me and called out to announce my presence.

'Thank God!' cried a tearful voice in reply. 'You've saved a life. I was going to gas myself.'

'I'm not far off it either,' I said.

Lesley was propped up in bed, in a state of near-hysteria, literally tearing her hair, with open textbooks scattered all around her. I pushed them aside to make room for myself. She gave a loud wail and cried noisily for some minutes. Then she recited formulas until I shut her up.

She's a wonderful girl. Warm-hearted, generous, the most undemanding person I've ever met. I never introduced her to my parents, though, because for all their so-called advanced views I was afraid they'd take her seriously and that was the last thing she wanted. Nor did I want Caroline to meet her, although she knew of her existence. I had no doubt that Lesley slept around quite a lot but I never asked her and she never mentioned it. All I knew was that she was always willing but she was not the least bit possessive and she never asked me anything either. I didn't want to tell her anything about Janet, though, because I'd a feeling it could hurt her, which is odd if, as I truly believe, Lesley never cared for me at all seriously.

The trouble is that although one knows exactly what

one feels and which is the person who really matters for keeps, no woman ever seems to be able to understand this. They can't seem to take it in that you can love someone absolutely loyally, devotedly and permanently, and yet at the same time you can sleep with another girl and be grateful to her and like her. I'm sure I'm not peculiar in this; I'm sure I'm as normal as anyone.

Anyway, if any girl could understand this, Lesley would be that one and I shall never forget her that week-end, clinging to me and howling, suddenly pulling herself away to make a dive over the end of the bed at a textbook, holding it up in the air over my head and reading aloud, giving her short rather raucous laugh as she threw it back on the floor, and then flinging herself upon me again. It was the last time we lay together. I was soon to slip into a world where there was no place for her laughter and I never saw her again.

My last exam was on the Thursday afternoon. By Wednesday evening I was beginning to think of myself as part of the everyday world again and I even conde-scended to join the others at the dinner-table. In fact I was the most cheerful person present and more or less kept the conversation going. Caroline sat grimly silent, ate much less than usual and I learnt, for the first time, that in fact she had been unwell all the week. Janet didn't look at all bright either, and it seemed to me that she frequently glanced nervously at Caroline.

It looked as if something had been going on that I knew nothing about, but it didn't matter now, because there was only tomorrow to get through and then after that I would attend to everything. Janet and I were going to come out into the open; we were really going to enjoy ourselves and make plans for our future. As for Caroline, with nothing else on my mind I was going to take time off to keep a thorough watch on her to see whether in fact she did get up to any revolting practices and if she did then I was going to face her with it and insist that she should tell my father. She could make it an appeal for help; she didn't even need to say she was doing such things, only that she had an overwhelming urge to do them.

I'd got it all worked out. Of course I didn't talk about it at the dinner-table but I did hold forth about a lot of other things. My parents seemed to be rather preoccupied but once my mother put a hand on my arm and said: 'Dear Richard,' and once or twice my father smiled at me and asked what I proposed to do to celebrate my release the next day.

'Haven't quite decided yet,' I replied. But I had decided. I was going straight to the hospital to collect Janet, and this time there wasn't going to be any of that miserable intrigue. I got hold of Janet after Caroline had gone to bed and told her what I proposed.

'Won't you be rather done in by then?' she asked doubtfully.

'Not too much for an evening with you. You're not still thinking of that stupid business – you know what.'

'Oh no. That's forgotten. But I thought perhaps we might wait till Saturday —'

'Well of course if you don't *want* to come out with me —'

'Oh Richard, I do, I *do*!'

Her eyes filled with tears. I caught her by the shoulders. 'What *is* the matter, Jan? There's something going on here. I don't like it. Is Caroline being very bitchy to you?'

She gave a sob, controlled herself with an effort and shook her head.

'That's it, of course,' I said. 'Damn her. *Damn* her.'

'It's no worse than usual,' muttered Janet, 'and she's really not been well. I'll be all right. Don't you worry about it, please.'

'I *am* going to worry about it. I'm going to get to-morrow over and then I'm going to sort out Caroline. Are you quite sure you'd rather I didn't collect you at hospital tomorrow evening?'

'Quite sure, honestly. I'd much rather come home. And you'll probably find you'd rather stay and talk to people afterwards for a bit. And then you can come home and sleep it all off and forget it, and after that we'll decide how to celebrate. How's that?'

I had to admit it sounded sensible. Very sensible and Janet-like.

'It's only one more day, though,' I concluded, 'and then I'm going to take you all in hand. I'm really going to get down to it.'

'Dear Richard.' She touched my arm in the very way my mother had done. 'Good night. Sleep well and good luck for tomorrow.'

I didn't sleep well though. I wasn't terribly concerned about my last paper, which would be more or less a case of coasting along on the momentum already gained by churning out facts day after day. I think it was the way that both my mother and Janet had spoken to me that made me uneasy, though I had no idea why this should be so. Or perhaps it is always the case that, looking back after an event, one imagines one had a premonition of it.

The day passed. I came out of the building with a feeling of staleness rather than of relief and went off with some of the others for a drink as Janet had predicted. I didn't want to particularly. All I wanted to do was to sleep, but there were several hours to get through before one could decently do that and it was probably easier to get through some of them in a sort of communal depression than in total aimlessness at home. I wouldn't have wanted any sort of an evening out. Janet was quite right about that too.

6

I GOT home shortly after seven, found a parking place for the mini, which my mother had let me have full use of for the exam weeks, and noticed that Dad's Zephyr didn't seem to be anywhere in the street. Of course parking is pretty hopeless and it was possible that he had had to go round the corner, but none the less I was conscious of a vague sense of disappointment. I had thought he was going to be home early that evening and if I felt any interest in anything whatsoever at that moment, it was in having a general survey of the whole of Finals with him. So I turned the key in the lock feeling even more low-spirited and very nearly tripped over the wheel of Caroline's chair.

'What the hell —'

She struggled to her feet with her twisted, laborious movements, and threw herself at me.

'Thank God you've come! Oh Dickie, Oh Dickie!'

She began to scream at the top of her voice, with complete abandon. I lifted her back into the chair.

'What is it? What's the matter? Where's everyone? Where's Mother?' I asked in a rush as soon as I could make myself heard.

'Out. They're all out. There's no one here. I'm terrified. Terrified.'

She began to scream again. I thought desperately of sedatives. Dared I give her anything? How did I know she hadn't taken something already? Best get the doctor, quick. I did my best to soothe her as I pushed her along to her room and lifted her on to the bed.

'Hush, Carol. You'll be all right. I'll get the doctor. He won't be long.'

But her arms clung round my neck and she broke into a storm of weeping.

'Are you in pain? Are you ill?'

She made no reply except to say again and again: 'I'm terrified, terrified.'

'Look, dear, I can't help if you don't try and tell me what it is. They wouldn't have left you alone for long – you know we never do. I expect Dad'll be in any moment. And anyway, where's Janet? She's usually home long before this.'

Caroline began to scream again. 'Janet! Janet! She's left – gone away!'

I felt suddenly chill inside. 'Gone away? What d'you mean? Where's she gone?'

I had to wait while she controlled her sobs. My fingers were itching to shake her. My arm was round her shoulders and my muscles were cramped with the strain of not gripping too hard. At last she spoke.

'I don't know where. She went out without saying anything. About an hour ago, I think. It seems like ten.'

I felt a slight sense of relief. Caroline was almost certainly lying. If Janet had really been left in charge of her then she wouldn't have gone anywhere for more than a very few minutes at the outside. She had gone round to the pillar-box, perhaps, or to one of the local shops that stayed open late. Or maybe Caroline had been so intolerable to her that she felt she must get out of the flat for a minute or two or burst. Or it might even be – and this seemed the most likely of all so I said it aloud to Caroline – that Janet had been trying without success to contact the doctor and had decided to hurry round to the surgery instead.

'It's sometimes quicker than hanging on the phone,' I added. 'I'm sure that's where she's gone. When did you begin to feel ill?'

She went off into hysterics again and I tried in vain to quieten her. In the intervals of her screaming I thought I heard someone come into the flat.

'There she is!' I cried. 'That's her coming in now!'

I succeeded in disentangling myself from Caroline and rushed to the front door. I wanted so much for it to be Janet that for a second I thought I saw her, but in fact it was my parents, coming in together, my mother holding tight to my father's arm.

'Where on earth have you been?' It burst out of me in furious reproach. 'I've just got in and found Caroline all alone and in hysterics saying Janet's gone out and she doesn't know where —'

My mother stepped forward and touched my arm. 'Janet can't have gone far,' she said. 'She'll be back in a moment. I'll go and see to Caroline. Tell him about it, will you, Andrew? It doesn't matter now.'

She smiled at me reassuringly and disappeared down the corridor. Still blazing, I followed my father into the consulting-room.

'And just what is this that I am now to be "told"?'

'Take it easy, lad, take it easy,' he said. 'It was your mother's wish, not mine. There was a very real danger that she was going to have to undergo a very serious operation, but I am thankful to say that the opinion we have sought this afternoon is considerably more favour-able and there is every possibility that it will not be necessary after all.'

He sank back into the chair he uses when he sees

patients. He had spoken in the most slick and pompous of Harley Street voices, but I knew it was only a cover-up for his own anxiety and my anger ebbed away.

'I'm sorry, Dad. I mean I'm pleased – pleased that it's not as bad as you feared.' I had to swallow hard before I could speak again. It came over me all at once. My poor mother. Here I'd been worrying away about everyone, including myself, making all sorts of plans to put every-one in their place, but with not a thought of Mother. And she'd had this hanging over her for weeks, apparently, and my father too.

Mother to be so ill. It had never happened before. I suppose, like everyone else until it actually happens, I had simply been taking it for granted that Mother would never get ill – that she'd go on for ever running around and doing things and fussing over everybody.

My father explained in rather more detail. I only hoped he was speaking the truth when he said she really was going to recover.

'I wish you'd told me before,' I said.

'I wanted to do so,' was his quiet reply. 'I'm not surprised you are annoyed. I would have felt the same in your place. But she was afraid it would affect your exams and it would have been too cruel to her to insist.'

I walked once more round the room.

'Does Caroline know?'

'No, and it will probably be best to say nothing to her for the moment. There has been some difficulty about my taking your mother to see Dr Fairlight this afternoon, but we were able to invent a little white lie and Caroline thinks your mother was very keen to hear a lecture I was giving and that's why she was out. Janet has been most helpful. We had to tell her because we needed her help and it was arranged that she should come home at lunch-time and stay with Caroline and I made it all right with Matron.'

For just one fraction of a second I had the thought: you ought to have told Caroline, you ought to have given her the chance to show her strength and be adult and responsible, but it was almost instantly superseded by my anxiety for Janet.

'Where *is* she?' I cried. 'She's been gone a long time now. Have you seen her at all today? What time did you and Mother have to go?'

'About half past three. Janet came home to lunch. She was perfectly all right. Caroline was going to have a rest and then take her books round to the gardens. And Janet asked if she could have the use of the kitchen because she wanted to do some cake-making in honour of your release.'

My father looked at me with slightly raised eyebrows as he said this, which I realised was his way of enquiring whether there was in fact anything between Janet and myself, but I was so disturbed by what he had said that I didn't take it up directly.

'She knew about Mother all the time, then,' I said. 'That explains a lot. And she's been at home with Caroline all afternoon.'

The chill feeling had come back in full force.

'It is rather odd, I must admit, that she should have been gone so long,' said my father. 'Unless she happened to see us arriving on her way back and realised there was no need for her to hurry home. No, that's nonsense,' he added before I could express my own contempt for the theory, 'she'd want to know at once the news of your mother.'

'Yes,' I said briefly. Yet again I circled the room. 'Look, Dad, I'm worried. I'm worried sick. I've got to tell you something. I ought to have told you before. I've got to tell you —'

'I think I had better go and see Caroline now,' said my father getting to his feet.

I reached the door before him and blocked his way. 'Caroline's all right for the moment. Mother knows how to deal with her. Dad – don't go and talk to her yet. Please let me tell you first!'

We stood staring at each other. We are both well over six foot but I think I am a trifle the bigger. It seemed a long time before he passed a hand across his eyes in the way he does when he is very exhausted and said in a low, drained voice:

'All right. Sit down and tell me.'

I think he must have had some sort of inkling even before I began. He listened without speaking a word, slumped in his chair, his elbow propped on the desk, his hand shading his eyes.

'I ought to have told you at once,' I said again. 'It's much worse than your not saying anything about Mother.'

Then it came out in a rush. It wasn't difficult at all, but when I had finished and my father at last raised his head I felt that I couldn't look at him.

'You've no doubt that was what you saw her doing?' he asked tonelessly.

'I had none at the time. It was only afterwards, when I began to think it over. It seemed so – so impossible. I thought I must have imagined it.'

'And you came straight in to me and I naturally thought you were suffering from a severe attack of pre-examination nerves. I don't see how I could possibly have guessed what really lay behind it, Richard.'

'Of course not.' It moved me terribly and yet at the

same time made me feel somehow ashamed to hear my father excusing himself. 'I ought to have told you. I very nearly did, only —'

I broke off. He covered his eyes again.

'Only you were afraid I would be very distressed by the communication. You were quite right. The impulses are there, of course. I have always been very much aware of that. I confess I hadn't suspected that they might be actually breaking through into her behaviour. You think it wasn't the first time?'

'I'm sure it wasn't, Dad. It was like – it was like a sort of regular ritual. And I couldn't help wondering what else – what other creatures – I mean she sits so absolutely quiet and motionless in her chair sometimes and then moves so rapidly —'

My father got to his feet, thrust his hands into his pockets and began to move about the room.

'Now let's get this straight. You believe you have discovered that Caroline is capable of inflicting actual physical torture as well as using verbal weapons. We all know that she can be bitterly jealous and that she is particularly possessive towards yourself. You are usually admirably careful to keep any legitimate objects of her jealousy well out of her reach, but Janet's coming to live here naturally put her under additional strain. I have not been entirely unaware of that, believe me, and I thought it over very seriously before deciding that Janet needed a home so badly that it was worth taking the risk. I knew I could rely on your full co-operation in this respect, although as I recollect I did in fact once remind you —'

'Please, Dad. Please, *please*!'

It burst out of me. I believe I even stretched out my hands to him in supplication. I know he was only working off his own terrible hurt but I think I could have borne it better if it had been an actual blow.

'It's all my fault,' I went on. 'I do love Janet and I haven't been careful enough and you can flay me as much as you like later on if it helps but please, *please* let's do something about it quickly, now.'

He covered his eyes again. 'Yes. Let's think. You're suspecting that Caroline has taken advantage of our absence to be so unkind to Janet that she has driven her out of the flat?'

'Yes. If not even worse,' I muttered.

'My dear boy, how could it be worse? We've got to keep our sense of proportion. Caroline may have goaded her temporarily beyond endurance or even perhaps have amused herself by sending Janet on some fool's errand – don't let's lose sight of that possibility, but she can't possibly have been the means of bringing Janet to any actual harm. Caroline's physical capacities are only too limited whereas Janet is a perfectly healthy young woman. She is under strain and is naturally still nervous from her experiences but she's perfectly capable of protecting herself.' He smiled faintly. 'Our Janet is no poor feeble little bird.'

I felt reassured. My father's idea of a hoax hadn't occurred to me and indeed it was just the sort of nasty thing that Caroline might do. We talked a few minutes longer and then he agreed to tackle Caroline while I had a look around Janet's room and elsewhere to see whether there was any clue to indicate why she had gone out.

I'm sure Dad did his best with Caroline, but he came away from her looking puzzled and worried and confessed that he hadn't been able to get any useful information out of her at all. Janet had made some biscuits and then they had had tea, according to Caroline. She,

Caroline, had then returned to her room because she felt too tired to go into the gardens. They hadn't been talking much over tea. Janet had been preoccupied and even sulky and she, Caroline, didn't see why she should put herself out to make conversation. She'd needed her pills after tea and had asked Janet to get them for her, but Janet had never brought them, and she supposed Janet had gone to her room or to watch television.

About à quarter to six she had felt well enough to get up and go and watch the news and was surprised to see that Janet wasn't there. When the news was over and she had still heard nothing of Janet she began to be worried and went to look for her. Janet was not in her room. With rising anxiety – so Caroline said – she went right through the flat. No sign of Janet anywhere, no note, no anything. She went right round again, in a panic this time, and eventually settled just inside the front door, hoping somebody would soon come in, and wondering whether she ought to try to call a neighbour, phone the police, or what. And that was that.

'It could be true,' concluded my father. 'She is certainly very upset.'

'But she's been alone before and not panicked like this!' I cried. 'Why didn't she go across the foyer and ring the Andersons' bell if she felt all that bad? Mrs Anderson would have taken her in till someone came home. Caroline knows that.'

My father was obliged to admit it.

'She's got a guilty conscience,' I continued. 'I bet that's why she's in such a state. She's sent Janet off on a wild-goose chase – told her there was a message to go and meet you – something like that.'

'In that case she'll be coming back as soon as she finds it was a hoax,' said my mother quietly.

We had had to tell her everything. She was taking it very well and had helped me look around Janet's room. 'I do hope she won't be very late,' went on my mother. 'It looks as if she's gone out without a coat – I don't think any are missing – and she'd only a thin frock on.'

'There's nothing gone but her handbag,' I added. 'The light brown one she usually carries.'

'Then she can't have intended to be away long,' said my father, 'and I really don't see that we can do anything much for the moment. She is adult and in her right mind. It's certainly extremely odd and unlike Janet but there must be some perfectly reasonable explanation. There is no point in speculating and we shall learn it eventually.'

'She might have been run over,' I exclaimed suddenly. This was a new idea, horrible enough but no more so than the thought that Caroline had been tormenting her.

'If she has then we shall be hearing from the police.'

'Can't we ring them now?'

I saw my parents exchange glances as I uttered these words.

'What do you think, Andrew?' asked my mother.

'Let's give it till ten,' was the reply.

Another half-hour. This was vaguely comforting, as setting a fixed time limit usually is, and my mind had become conditioned to living by the clock during my exams. It was just bearable to think of living through the next half-hour.

'I'll have another go at Caroline meanwhile,' I said.

They both stepped forward to detain me, my father first.

'Not now. She's asleep. At least we hope so.'

'I don't think you'd get any more sense out of her tonight, dear,' added my mother more gently.

I was disappointed but had to give in. Then I had

another idea, another way of getting through the next half-hour. 'I'm going out,' I said. 'Shan't be long.'

I think they protested but I didn't stop to listen. I did a sprint along to the gardens and pulled up short at the group of shrubs where Caroline sits. I don't know what I expected to find, but in my bemused state I could see clearly only one thing: nothing on earth would have induced Janet to go willingly out of the flat without leaving a note or sending a message to spare us distress and anxiety, and if she hadn't gone out in accordance with her own decision, then somehow Caroline must be at the back of it. I slumped down upon the garden bench. There was no one else about. It was a heavy dusk – had been dull and cloudy all day. There was very little sunshine, that spring and early summer. I kicked at the stones in the gravel and tried to imagine myself into Caroline's state of mind.

Here she had sat and pulled a living sparrow to pieces. This must be what she would like to do to Janet; perhaps to me, perhaps to others too. But was it simply a beastly equivalent of sticking pins into an image of one's enemy, or did it augur something worse? Janet's no feeble little bird, my father had said. True, but she was very full of conscience and sympathy; she could be only too easily played upon. My father had said 'don't speculate', but how could one possibly avoid it? Every conceivable variety of cruel hoax went through my mind, the most insistent being the idea that Caroline had known about Mother's illness after all, and had pretended to Janet that there had been a telephone message saying that Mother was desperately ill and she was to go at once.

That didn't explain why Janet had taken no coat, this cool and clammy evening, and it was even stranger that she had left no note in the flat. But if she thought it was

my parents sending for her, and if she had assumed that
Caroline would give me the message when I came in . . .
But what had Caroline hoped for except a few hours'
worry for Janet? And how could she possibly think her
ruse wouldn't be discovered? And why had she been so
very hysterical on my arrival? The more I thought about
it the more I became convinced that that, at least, was
genuine and not the act that might have been suspected.

I got up from the seat. My father was right. This sort
of speculation only made one more feverish than ever
and in any case it would soon be time to ring the police.

Inspector Soames was a tall, grey, middle-aged man
with melancholy eyes and a quiet manner. We were
apparently indebted for the honour of having him call in
person rather than send a subordinate, to the fact that he
had read some of my father's books and was an admirer
of his. After a few compliments they got down to the
business in hand. This took some time to sort out owing
to the fact that there had apparently been some error in
handing on our message, and the Inspector had been
under the impression that it was a young child who was
missing and not a young adult.

There had been one or two attacks on children in our
area recently, not fatal but unpleasant enough, and
people suspected the floating population of tramps and
hippies who inhabited the disused railway sidings the
other side of the canal. The Inspector explained about the
molesting of children, and while my father was putting
the record right my mind wandered on to a fresh track:
some of these types from the no-man's land would
wander over into Caroline's gardens from time to time.
Was it possible that she had established a relationship
with some of them? Was this another facet of her life in

the gardens that we knew nothing of and if so, was it conceivable that she had plotted with them to arrange for Janet's disappearance? A kidnapping? Had she held out the hope of a ransom? I felt cold again while I thought of it. I tried to shrug it off by remembering Brian's amused remarks about schemes for abduction but the idea would not leave me. I would mention it somehow or other – but without bringing in Caroline – before the Inspector left.

'Couldn't your niece have gone to see a friend?' he was asking my father. 'Have you been in touch with any people she is likely to have visited?'

My father appealed to me. 'Janet doesn't go visiting anywhere on her own, does she, Richard?'

'Never,' I said emphatically. 'She doesn't know anybody in London except us and the people at the hospital. She has lunch with them and sometimes stops a bit late after work to go and talk to some of the patients but she's never been by herself to visit anyone in their homes since she came to live with us.'

The Inspector still looked sceptical. 'Boy friends?' he asked, addressing himself largely to me.

'She doesn't have any,' I declared with vehemence. He studied me for a moment and it was impossible to tell what was going on behind those sad brown eyes.

'That's rather odd, isn't it?' he said and picked up the snapshot of Janet that we had taken from an album of family photographs found in her room. 'Nice looking girl.' He looked at me again.

My father once more explained her circumstances.

'She had friends at her old home, though, presumably,' said the Inspector.

Well, yes, we supposed so. Both Dad and I looked taken aback and slightly foolish at this question. Janet didn't often mention her former life and I'm afraid we had rather taken it for granted that she would cut herself off from it. I knew there were one or two girls whom she corresponded with and in whom I felt not the least interest, but I had never heard her refer to any boys. Some very unpleasant sensations began to arise within me and mingled with the anxiety.

'Mother might know,' I said.

My father reluctantly went to fetch her. Caroline was now in a deep drugged sleep and my mother had gone to rest, if not to sleep. I thought to take advantage of my father's short absence to put forward the kidnapping idea, feeling that I could better bear to have it brushed aside by the Inspector rather than by my father, but I got no chance because the Inspector had his own ideas of how to use these few minutes.

'Is there anything between your cousin and yourself that might account for her not coming home?' he asked mildly. 'Some understanding between you, followed by a quarrel maybe?'

I suppose it was a reasonable enough assumption, but it rather irritated me.

'No quarrel at all,' I said. 'She wished me good luck with my exams and we were going to have a little celebration when they were over.'

But she wouldn't come out with me this evening, I thought, although I didn't say it aloud. Was that only because of Mother's visit to the specialist or did she have another motive too? Had she just hung on until the end of my exams and then decided to solve the problem of Caroline and us all by simply disappearing? Was it after all entirely her own idea?

'But she was cooking – making cakes,' I exclaimed aloud in answer to my own unspoken questions. 'She was making lemon biscuits.' It was true; they were there in the kitchen. Surely that was evidence enough that she hadn't intended to go?

'They're my favourites,' I added and then I couldn't say any more. My eyes were pricking and I got up and went and sat at my father's desk and leaned my face on my hand just as he had done earlier.

My mother added her quota of information but it wasn't very relevant. Yes, Janet had spoken to her of several boys she used to know in York. One of them, Terence by name, seemed to be mentioned at first with some regret, but later on Janet had stated that her friend Mavis appeared to have annexed him so that, said my mother, was evidently that. She then added, what up till now had not been mentioned, the possibility that Janet had gone off following an actual quarrel with Caroline, and my father interposed quickly to say that we had no evidence of that except the fact that Caroline was very distressed.

The Inspector looked up at that point and glanced at us each in turn with the resigned air of one who is used to being told lies but doesn't always think it advisable to say so.

'Well, as you prefer not to disturb your daughter at the moment there's not much more we can do about that now,' he said, putting away his notebook and getting to his feet. 'I'll get the description out and check with casualty departments. And if you should hear anything meanwhile —'

'Naturally we will inform you immediately,' said my father.

I still hadn't mentioned the kidnapping idea. Mother followed Inspector Soames to the door and I came after.

'You don't think there's any danger that Janet may

have been attacked?' I heard her ask, and felt very grateful to her. 'I mean – these poor little children – might it not be an older girl too? I mean with all those tramps around —'

'No, madam, I think it is unlikely in the extreme,' said Inspector Soames. 'In fact I do not think they have anything whatever to do with the molesting of children either. It's not their line of country at all. I've a pretty shrewd suspicion who is responsible, and the individual I have in mind would not be the least interested in your niece. It's someone more in *your* province, sir.' He turned to my father. 'Not the very worst kind of sex offender but bad enough. I was very interested, by the way, in what you were saying on that television programme the other night about new developments in drug therapy for psychopaths —'

They moved through the hall, talking amicably. I could have hit them both. I was filled with a great sense of anti-climax, a huge and hopeless void. Sending round a description and asking the hospitals about road accidents. It seemed to me a wretched, footling bit of activity. I don't know what I'd been hoping for. Full-scale searches, I suppose; tracker dogs and the army and the lot.

My mother sensed my disappointment. 'It's very much routine business to him, dear,' she said. 'People go missing all the time and soon turn up again. For all sorts of reasons. Usually they go missing because they want to, I believe.'

'Janet didn't want to go. Oh Mother!'

I dropped down on to the floor by her chair and began to howl like a baby. She didn't say anything at all; she must have been tired beyond anything.

My father came back and put a hand under her arm to

help her rise. 'You'd better go to bed too, Richard,' he said. 'Have you some more of those capsules?'

'I don't want any more dope,' I cried wildly. 'I'm going to sit up. There's got to be someone awake in case Janet comes home.'

I saw them look at each other and their faces were grey and old. It was the way they had looked when we first knew that Caroline would never walk again. They didn't try to argue and they didn't try to say anything reassuring; they simply said 'Goodnight then,' and left the room. But it was as clear as if they had sat there talking for hours that this time they were looking like that because of me.

7

JANET didn't come back that night. Nor the next day, nor the day after, nor the day after that. Then it was Monday and the start of a new week, but it seemed to me that the sun had stopped still and the hands of the clock had ceased to move and there was no more time.

Mrs Dring came in to help afternoons as well as mornings. My mother started her treatment and I drove her to the Clinic and waited there and then brought her back. It was depressing and painful and she didn't try to conceal this from me. We talked about her illness and we talked about myself and Janet and also about Caroline. She knew a lot more than I had ever realised she did about Caroline. She too had been apprehensive about Janet's coming but had apparently also decided that it was the lesser of two evils because of Janet's overwhelming need for a home.

'It would be so much better if only Dad would insist on Caroline going for proper treatment,' she said wistfully. My mind was still running on her own recent ordeal at the Clinic and at first I misunderstood her.

'Good God!' I cried, appalled at the notion that I might have to dredge up yet more pity, 'don't tell me there's something *else* the matter with Caroline!'

We were stationary at traffic lights; I glanced sideways at her. She looked very unhappy but also slightly alarmed and she did not reply.

'Oh, of course,' I went on, realising then what she was referring to. 'Of course – psychiatric treatment for Caroline. I thought Dad was going to do something about it.'

The traffic moved on. My mother said nothing more and I could understand her silence. She loves my father very dearly and she does her best to understand and respect his work, but there is a little hard core inside her that considers mental illness a disgrace, something that happens to other people. It would be terribly hard for her to admit that it could ever apply to her own children. So I didn't mention it again. In fact I didn't want to think of Caroline as being in need of medical help at all, so certain was I that she was responsible for my losing Janet and so determined was I to get the truth out of her when she should be capable of answering questions. She developed a high fever after that first night and was scarcely able to speak. The fever was real enough and our local G.P. was sent for and she was generally made a fuss of. I put my head round the door of her room from time to time and when she seemed a little better promised to look out some new thrillers for her. But I couldn't feel much sympathy.

I couldn't feel anything much. Inspector Soames came again and his questions began to take on a very definite slant. What was the exact degree of injury Miss Packington had suffered? Had she fully recovered? Was the depression following the death of her parents particularly severe? Had she shown any signs of wishing to end it all? And so on. It was nonsense and I said as much. Janet had been through a very unhappy time but she was getting over it and she certainly hadn't gone off on that Thursday afternoon in order to take her own life. She was waiting anxiously to hear the result of her aunt's interview with the specialist and she had baked some of her cousin's favourite cakes and would want to have the satisfaction of seeing him eat them.

At this point Inspector Soames had sighed audibly

'It's a pity Miss Duncan isn't able to help us. Is she often taken ill in this way?'

My father explained. 'I'll let you know when she's fit to talk,' he concluded, 'but I doubt very much whether she will be able to help.'

Nor was she. Eventually Caroline got up and sat in her chair again and received the Inspector in the consulting-room. He thought it best that none of us should be present, but we gathered that she had no more to tell him than she had told us already. She hadn't seen Janet since they had tea together about four-thirty and she hadn't heard her go out, but she wouldn't have heard the front door shut from her own room at the back of the flat. Janet had said nothing about her plans and they had scarcely talked over tea. There had been no quarrel, but they hadn't much in common with each other. As far as she knew there had been no ring at the bell and no telephone call during the time she and Janet were in the flat together, but it was possible that she had failed to hear something, because the two extensions were in the front of the flat and if Janet had picked up the receiver immediately the phone rang then Caroline would probably not have heard it.

It was very much as I had expected. There was no information to be got from Caroline; not by any conventional methods, anyway.

Meanwhile enquiries had been made of our neighbours, none of whom had seen Janet go out that afternoon. That was not unexpected either, and meant very little. We are not the sort of area where people sit behind net curtains and speculate on the activities of those around them. There are eight large flats in our block, mostly inhabited by hard-working professional people. I doubt if anyone ever glances out of a window except to see if it's raining, and the other side of the road is very similar. There is a little row of shops around the corner and the people there are rather more inquisitive and chatty and Janet seems to have been on friendly greeting terms with them. They weren't much help either, though. They had seen nothing of her that afternoon, but they had no view of the entrance to our block and she could equally well have gone in the opposite direction to the tube station as to the bus-stop outside the shops.

If in fact she had left the building on foot at all; but there was no evidence to suggest that she had been called for in a car or taken a taxi. There was no sign of anything. The only positive clue of any sort that was found was when we were going through Janet's belongings – a hateful business and Mother wanted to do it by herself but I insisted on being present.

The cupboards and drawers revealed a careful and tidy nature but nothing else, and the photographs of her parents and former pets and the little bits of letters from friends in York nearly started me howling again. She *couldn't* have gone of her own free will; these treasures, at least, she'd have taken with her. My mother said that she was pretty sure that none of Janet's possessions were missing, and it was at that moment that I discovered the one clue. She had a few books propped up between bookends on top of the chest-of-drawers and there was a neat pile of magazines lying beside them.

The memory of the evening when I had discovered her practising shorthand returned to me with a painful stab and I wondered for the first time since her disappearance whether she had continued to hide her exercise book. There was no sign of it, nor of the little blue textbook, either between the bookends or among the magazines. I told my mother about it and we went through the whole room inch by inch. Even the Inspector was impressed by the thoroughness of our search. The shorthand books were missing, along with the clothes she had been wearing and the light brown shoulder bag that she usually carried and that was well known to us because she would often have it with her even when she was moving about the flat.

The Inspector took note of the missing books and my mother looked puzzled but advanced various theories for their disappearance. Perhaps, once Janet had felt herself to be quite competent, she had simply thrown them away; perhaps she had taken them to her office at the hospital to refer to there; perhaps she had lent them to another girl at the hospital. These last two theories were quickly disproved on enquiry, but the first one was capable of no proof.

Inspector Soames suggested that we might see whether the books were anywhere else in the flat, which I had been intending to do in any case. In a home like ours, however, such a search was no easy task. My father's library, mostly kept in the consulting-room, runs into a good few thousands, and both Caroline and I have bulging bookcases. Even my mother is a bit of a hoarder when it comes to books, only she can never decide where to keep them and is always starting up fresh little outcrops of paperbacks all over the flat.

However, I didn't propose to go hunting religiously through the lot until after I had followed up a hunch of my own. I didn't believe Janet had killed herself; I didn't believe she had been the victim of some homicidal maniac; and it had been established that she had not been killed or injured in a road accident. I refused to let myself think that she was not alive and I had at last succeeded in taking my father's advice not to indulge in pointless speculation. Up till now I had been sure of only one thing: that Caroline knew something about Janet's disappearance, but now I had something more; I had the definite fact of the missing shorthand books. It was not just idle speculation to put the two together and to suspect that Caroline knew something about the missing books too.

I thought it advisable to let Mother mention the missing books to Caroline while I watched her reactions. There seemed to be some sort of telepathy between my mother and myself at the time and we knew, without speaking, what the other wanted done. I didn't even have to put the idea into Mother's head. She mentioned it casually over dinner. Caroline had been up for several days and was, physically at least, back to her normal self again.

'I don't suppose you know where they are, do you, darling?' my mother asked.

Caroline had a spoonful of soup half-way to her mouth. It might have been too hot and she might have changed her mind and decided to take another mouthful of bread before the soup, but I was watching her expression very closely and I think she was startled by the question and that it was to give herself a chance to recover that she put the spoon down and broke the bread.

'Shorthand?' she said disdainfully after a moment's pause. 'What should *I* want with shorthand?'

This gave me my chance. 'It's rather useful,' I said. 'Saves time on all sorts of occasions. As a matter of fact' – and I looked her full in the face – 'as a matter of fact I've picked up the bulk of the theory and can read and write it pretty well myself.'

This time there was no doubt at all about the reaction. The red patches came out in her cheeks as they do when she is angry and she glared at me.

'Is this an insurance policy against failure to get your degree?' she asked nastily. 'Is this the only alternative method you can think of to earn your daily bread? Our fine Dickie! A little spotty clerk!'

My father roused himself. He had been silent and even morose since Janet's disappearance, speaking only when it was necessary and shutting himself up in his consulting-room for hours at a time.

'Actually,' he said, 'I once started to study shorthand myself. I wish I had persevered. It would have been most useful in taking notes from patients.' Having spoken, he sank back again into his thoughts and we continued the meal in silence.

'You haven't got Janet's books then?' said my mother presently.

Caroline looked at her and then turned her head away, not deigning to reply, and it only took the slightest flicker of an eyelid for me to convey to Mother that it was best to drop the subject now.

I felt a strong undercurrent of excitement at having at last got on the track of something and made a chink in Caroline's armour, but I had to be very careful not to spoil my chances by a premature and clumsy assault. Here again my mother seemed to be reading my thoughts and after dinner she begged me not to tackle Caroline on the matter.

'Leave it to me,' she said. 'I can use a little gentle blackmail. It'll be much easier for me. I won't find it quite so difficult to stay patient with her.'

It was my mother's way of telling me that she was afraid I was going to lose my temper. I didn't want her to have any more anxiety so I promised to do nothing unless she said so. I only hoped she believed me because in fact I had no intention whatever of leaving it to her.

Gentle blackmail would get nowhere. Caroline had too much at stake. There was one way only to make her talk and that was to frighten her into it. Her reactions to my probing over the dinner-table encouraged me in this belief.

My mother had to go to the Clinic the following afternoon and it so happened that Mrs Dring wanted to get off early to go to a grandchild's christening and there was some doubt as to whether she could wait until our return. It was therefore arranged that I should drive Mother there as usual but that she should take a taxi home, and this would avoid Caroline being left in the flat by herself. Mother was not happy about this arrangement and I could see that she had not complete faith in my promise.

'Now be careful, darling,' she said as we parted at the entrance to the Clinic, 'for my sake please be careful.' I knew she was not referring only to my driving home.

In fact I was dreadfully on edge and my driving was all over the place. Mrs Dring had tidied herself up and was ready to go when I got back.

'Where's Caroline?' I asked.

'She's resting.' Her big plain face was sombre and she looked at me curiously. 'I'd leave her be if I was you.'

'Why? What's the matter with her, Mrs D.?'

'We're having one of our bad days. I'd leave her be till the Doctor comes home. I've put your tea ready in the kitchen. It only needs the kettle boiling.'

'Thanks,' I said vaguely, 'thanks,' and I moved across the hall to Janet's room and then turned round again.

'Why don't you watch the cricket?' said Mrs Dring, still hovering at the front door. 'It's not always the waiting-room's free.'

'Oh yes.' I came back across the hall. 'Maybe I will.'

She looked at me again, shook her head, and let herself out.

I glanced at myself in the mirror that hangs over the table in the hall. Why had Mrs Dring looked at me so oddly? Did I look like the Third Murderer? As far as I could see there was nothing unusual about my reflection. It wasn't exactly beaming with *joie de vivre* but on the other hand I am the possessor of an appearance of such rude health that it would take more than a week or so of ghastly anxiety to produce a noticeable dent in it.

All the same, the old girl had seemed to be wanting to warn me. Very decent of her, but surely unnecessary. If there was one person in this world whom Caroline could not harm, whom she could neither frighten by her venom and her tantrums nor soften with her weakness and her weeping, that one was myself. I wasn't going to be put off; I wasn't going to be made to feel guilty; I was going to get the truth out of her. I knew I could do it and that nobody else could.

When we were children, long before Caroline became ill, I'm afraid I sometimes used to bully her. I'm not very proud of it, but I suppose all elder brothers do so at some time or another and I certainly had plenty of provocation. At times she would drive me beyond endurance by taunting me with my stupidity over my homework and I would threaten to break her arm if she didn't shut up. She eased off a little as we grew older, while I became both more thick-skinned and more self-controlled and of course after her paralysis everything was different. But I was going to force myself to forget that now. She deserved no special consideration; she'd sheltered behind her disability for long enough. I was going to get the truth out of her, gently if possible, brutally if necessary.

I think she had an inkling of my intentions. I think it was she who had put Mrs Dring up to trying to keep me away from her. I found her lying on her bed, propped up against high pillows, which was the most comfortable position for her to rest, with her eyes closed and a tartan rug drawn up to her waist, covering her useless legs. Her arms, which had escaped the ravages of the disease, were folded outside the rug, the hands tucked behind the elbows. She was only pretending to be asleep.

'Carol,' I said softly.

She stirred a little, sighed, and settled her head in a fresh position. I pulled a chair up to the bed, sat down, laid my right hand lightly on her left arm and felt it tremble.

'You're not asleep, Carol. I know you're not.'

'Do go away,' she murmured without opening her eyes. 'I've had a rotten night. I feel bloody awful.'

'So have I. So do I.'

Her eyes opened. They were dark pools of hopelessness and pain.

'You,' she said in a low voice full of loathing. 'You – feel – bloody awful! You! You don't know what suffering is.'

'Perhaps not. But I'm beginning to learn,' I replied equally quietly. 'That's what you wanted, wasn't it?'

She continued to look at me but said nothing.

'Carol,' I said, 'why did you take Janet's shorthand books out of her room?'

'Oh, my God, are you still on at that?'

'Yes. Why did you take them?'

We stared at each other. She tried to move her hand away and I let it go. I was very interested in what it was going to do, in what it might tell me. I remembered how Janet had sat down on top of the bedclothes that covered the books she didn't want me to find. If Caroline wanted to hide something but at the same time to have ready access to it herself, she would conceal it either in her bed or in her wheelchair. My eyes moved to the latter; there were a couple of cushions on it. I got up and moved them and then replaced them again. No shorthand books there; she must be lying on them then. Under the rug perhaps, or under the pillow, or even down between the bed-clothes.

I went and sat beside her again. I wanted her to give in without any threat of force. In spite of my resolution I was beginning to feel a loathing of myself. Frightening and threatening a sick and helpless woman. Whatever the motive, it was a foul thing to do. I prayed that she would answer my question.

Her arms shifted slightly but it was only to fold them-themselves the tighter. They were giving me no clue. And then at last she spoke, wearily, her voice full of contempt.

'You are every possible sort of a swine, aren't you, Richard Duncan. All right. I did swipe the books. I wanted to study shorthand. For a reason of my own. And now will you kindly leave me in peace.'

Her head dropped back again on the pillow and her eyes closed.

'Where are they now?' I asked.

'I'll give them to you this evening.'

'I want to know where they are now.'

'All right. I heard you the first time. Don't you want to know why I wanted to learn shorthand?'

I certainly did, but was sure she was raising the point at this moment only to distract my attention.

'I want those books now,' I said, not getting up from my chair but watching her every movement.

'Oh God!' She gave a little moan and began with

98

slow, awkward movements to shift herself about on the bed. I had to look away. My fingers were gripping tightly to the sides of the chair on which I was sitting in the effort of stopping myself from holding out a helping hand.

Suddenly, in her efforts to move sideways and, for all I knew, to get off the bed, her right arm seemed to slip on the pillow and she tilted over towards the wall, away from where I was sitting. She remained in this uncomfortable and twisted position for a moment or two, swearing softly. I held my breath and forced myself to say nothing and to make no move. It was the sort of minor mishap that could happen to her at any time and retard still further her laborious progress. But it might equally well have been a skilful feint. I couldn't see round her to the top end of the bed beside the wall and I couldn't see what her right hand was doing. It might have been simply struggling to find a firm enough grip on the pillows to push her up again; it might have been doing something else.

I waited. It was becoming ever more difficult to be patient, but if I was going to gain anything, that would be the way. There was no point in picking her up and grabbing the books, if indeed she had them there. It wasn't only the books that I wanted, but her whole attitude towards them that I needed to know.

She heaved herself even farther round to face the wall and her left arm moved across too. It emerged again to lay a small blue object on the tartan rug. The process was repeated with the exercise book. She steadied herself on her right elbow, turned herself once more on to her back and collapsed against the pillows. They had slipped during her movements and she was no longer propped up so high, but her eyes were closed, her face was deathly pale, and she lay with her arms folded over the rug just as she had done when I came in. The two books were tilted up against the ridge formed by her legs.

'There you are,' she muttered, barely opening her lips. 'Now go away.'

But this wasn't the end. It was only the start.

I picked up the textbook and flipped over the pages. It looked exactly as it had done when I had read out passages from it to Janet. The exercise book was about half-full of neatly inscribed squiggles, with every now and then a cross in the margin where she had made a mistake. I turned the pages slowly. The outlines became stronger and more confident and the crosses in the margin fewer. For the last dozen or so pages there were no crosses at all. I read a few lines at random; it wasn't all that difficult. I'd been learning with her and had helped to correct her exercises.

'We have received your communication of the 6th instant and note that you require a further estimate to be submitted —'

Terrible stuff. Why couldn't they put something a bit more lively into it now and again?

It was all pretty much the same, but near the end of the written pages I recognised a passage that we had worked on together, a short report including some medical terms. I had said at the time that at last we'd got to something that would be of use to her and Janet had taken particular care over that section. After that it reverted to the 'yours of the 5th to hand' rubbish and then the blank pages began. Evidently she hadn't troubled to do much work after dismissing me from her service, but then she hadn't needed to by then. All the signs were made in Janet's writing up to the end. Shorthand-writing embraces as many varieties of hand, and is subject to as many personal idiosyncrasies, as is ordinary handwriting, and I should think it is much harder to forge. I would have noticed at once had there been any entries written by another person. Whatever Caroline had been up to, she certainly had not been writing any exercises herself.

So that was one thing eliminated. Caroline had not been wanting to learn to write shorthand. She might say she had been using other bits of paper to write on, but in that case she would have to produce them, and in any case I thought this was unlikely. But if she didn't want to write, then she could be wanting the knowledge for only one thing, and that was to be able to read something written in shorthand.

I felt my heart quicken as I came to this conclusion. I was getting somewhere, I was sure, but it was becoming harder than ever to remain patient and bide my time.

To read shorthand. Not in order to decipher the 'Yours of the 5th' guff but to read something that mattered, to gain some knowledge that could not be gained in any other way. It must be something very important indeed to make her go to the length of concealing the books and trying to put us off the scent – much more important than Janet's pathetic little attempt to hide what she thought of as her own shortcomings.

I glanced at Caroline's pale face and motionless form. Did she really suppose I'd be satisfied now? Did she believe that I wouldn't be taking the matter further? It might well be that she did. She had a supreme contempt for my powers of reasoning. Right. Let her go on thinking me too dim to grasp the implications.

I looked back at the exercise book again and continued to think it out. There wasn't anything of significance in those pages. Once more I turned them over slowly. They were nothing but graded practice exercises. But Caroline didn't know that. Or even if she had learnt enough to know it now, she couldn't have known it when she started her studies. She must have suspected that there was something very important written in Janet's exercise book. What sort of thing? Admissions of love? A record of daily events? A young girl's thoughts on life? Bosh. A fat lot Caroline cared about what Janet thought about anything. Unless it was something really hot. True confession stuff. Caroline had a nice taste in pornography as well as crime. It was just conceivable that she believed Janet had kept some sort of diary and hoped to find something worth reading in it.

Oh rot! I shook myself impatiently. Not Janet. There could be no possible satisfaction for a taste like Caroline's in any innocent little confidences Janet might have to make. Unless it was I who was the innocent and Janet was nothing but a tart at bottom and they'd all realised it but been keeping quiet to spare my feelings. Rot, I said to myself again though I didn't use such a polite term this time; not my little Jan, not the girl who played with her dachshund, who was terribly embarrassed when I barged into her room when she was going to bed.

But that wasn't why she was bothered, came a nasty little voice that I hardly recognised as part of myself at all; she was only worrying about her backwardness with her shorthand. Maybe I'd disappointed her; maybe all my grim self-control had been totally unnecessary; maybe she'd given me up and gone to seek her pleasures else-where. My image of Janet was beginning to fade. Shut up, you fool, I told myself furiously; go on like that and you'll drive yourself mad – and there's enough of that here already, God knows. Whatever Janet may be, she's lost and has got to be found.

But the little voice would not be stilled: if she's like that, then I don't want her back in any case. I kicked at the thought; I hated it and was ashamed of it, but it wouldn't go away. And then it seemed as if Caroline and my mother and Lesley and others and even Janet herself rose up in a great regiment and cried sneeringly: Hypocrite! Double standard! But I can't *help* it, I protested to these unseen accusers; I *do* think it's different for men and women, I didn't make myself, I was born that way.

Suddenly all was quiet. This must be the monster, jealousy, I said to myself; that I could have lived so long without feeling how sharp was its bite, that was the miracle.

I am not a quick thinker, but all this had gone through my mind during the few minutes I sat by Caroline's bed, turning over the pages of the blue exercise book, while she lay absolutely still.

'Carol,' I said very softly, 'Carol – why did you want to learn to *read* shorthand?'

There was no reply, only the faintest flutter of the eyelids.

'How much have you learnt? Can you read what is written here?'

Still no answer.

'What did you think she'd written? What were you expecting to find?'

She stirred and turned her face to the wall. 'Leave me alone.'

'Were you hoping for a diary? Some nice juicy titbits? Some good hot stuff?'

This was a trap. I'd recovered my balance again and I had a good hope that she might fall into it. I waited in tense anxiety. She turned her face slowly towards me and opened her eyes.

'For your own sake, Dickie,' she said wearily, 'I advise you not to enquire further.'

I pressed my hands together between my knees. They were shaking with excitement. She'd fallen in. She'd been outwitted, probably for the first time in her life, and by her despised stupid brother too.

'So she did keep a diary, did she,' I said quietly. 'That's very interesting. I wonder how much of it you have managed to decipher?'

I saw the flash of panic in her eyes before she looked away. She had seen her error of course. She tried to retrieve it.

'I've got nowhere yet,' she said and her voice was trembling slightly. 'It's bloody awful stuff to learn.'

'Then how do you know anything about a diary?'

I continued to look closely into her face. She was silent for a moment and then she stretched out a hand and touched my arm – my mother's gesture. It seemed to burn through my sleeve but I didn't pull away.

'Richard,' she said in quiet confidential tones, 'you don't really know anything much about Janet, do you?'

'Perhaps not.'

'She's not really a little milk and water miss, you know.'

'Perhaps not,' I said again.

'I've heard her say things —' She stopped and hastily corrected herself. 'She has told Mother things and I've got them out of Mother – well, she's been a pretty quick worker considering how young she is.'

'A quick worker indeed,' I said, 'and a very determined one to overcome all the sheer physical problems that arise in trying to lead a life of promiscuity while living at home with parents or aunts and uncles. Very clever indeed. I wish *I* found it so easy.'

She must have known then that she had lost but she went on batting gamely.

'Of course you're out such a lot, so very wrapped up in yourself —'

I was beginning to get tired of this shadow boxing. 'Now, Carol, let's come to the point. Where is Janet's shorthand-written diary?'

'There,' she said and indicated with a movement of her eyes the blue exercise book that lay now on the floor by the bed.

I stood up, moved her paralysed legs to the side, and sat down on the edge of the bed. I could almost hear her cringing.

'No, it's not there,' I said. 'You know that perfectly well. It's written somewhere else. In another notebook. A smaller one probably. One that can be more easily hidden. What else have you got under that pillow, Caroline?'

I leaned forward, still not touching her. But she screamed then – a weird, bloodcurdling, animal shriek.

'Hurry up now,' I said roughly. 'Hand it over – or move aside and let me get it. You can move that much.'

She screamed again and then she began to swear at me – really filthy stuff. I tried not to hear it; I didn't want to know.

'Oh, for Christ's sake let's get this over with!'

I hadn't realised how strained I'd been. My nerves were at breaking point. I could stand no more. I caught hold of her arms just below the elbow. In a flash she ducked her head and sank her teeth into the middle finger of my right hand. I yelled in turn.

'You – bitch! You – you vampire!'

I let go her other arm and prised her jaws apart with my left hand. I'm pretty strong but even so it wasn't all that easy. Like interfering in a dog-fight. There was no possible way not to hurt her. I was making a hell of a mess of her face.

'Let go!' I cried. 'Don't be a fool! You haven't a chance! Are you trying to make me kill you?'

'Yes!' It came out in another long and horrifying banshee wail.

And then her teeth tried to snap at my left hand too. I got both thumbs under her chin and pushed her head back. Her hands clutched at me feebly and then dropped; her body went slack. I loosed my hold, felt under the pillow, and drew out a little red memo book, with ruled feint lines, small enough to slip into a pocket or handbag. I stood upright and dropped it into my jacket pocket.

And then the mists receded and I saw clearly what was before my eyes. Caroline lay slumped against the pillows. Her head was hanging sideways; her eyes were shut, her lower jaw was drooping; there were angry red patches all over her face and neck, and she didn't stir.

8

I BELIEVE I walked straight out of the room and down the corridor to the hall. I was going to telephone, I think. First the doctor and then the police. I was very calm – frozen calm – but all the time there was a voice going on inside my head: you've killed your sister, your sister who's a cripple; you've killed a paralysed woman; you've killed your sister. It hammered away as if the fact could never be repeated often enough: you've killed your crippled sister.

I was standing by the telephone table in the hall, turning up the pad to find the phone numbers for the doctor and the police, when there was a ring at the front door. In my half-crazy state I thought that I must have somehow slipped a whole section of time and that this would be them arriving already.

I opened the door. At first I didn't recognise the plump elderly woman who stood there panting slightly.

'I'm sorry to disturb you,' she said, 'I quite forgot – only found out when I was half-way there on the bus – forgot to put the christening mug in my bag after I showed it to your mother —'

She broke off suddenly. 'Why, Richard, Mr Richard! Whatever's the matter with your hand?'

I looked down at it. Where Caroline had bitten my finger I was dripping blood. There was a trail of it along the carpet.

'She went for me,' I said. 'I've killed her.'

The big plain face of Mrs Dring floated in front of me; I saw the eyes narrow. Then she said briskly:

'Nonsense. Of course you haven't. She's foxing. Playing you up. The little devil. I'll go and see.'

She went off down the corridor. I found a handkerchief and wrapped it round my finger. Then I dropped down on my knees and rubbed at the bloodstains in the light grey carpet – rubbed them farther in. I remained kneeling but sat back when Mrs Dring appeared again. She was panting more than ever.

'She's all – right,' she said with difficulty. 'Quite conscious – breathing – pulse steady. There's no need – to tell – anyone.'

She sank her bulk down upon the stool beside the telephone table. I wasn't aware of any relief. I wasn't aware of anything except anxiety for Mrs Dring. She was puffing away worse than ever and looked blue in the face. I got up and stood beside her. 'I'd better get a doctor for you,' I said.

She moved her hand slightly. She couldn't speak. A moment later she managed to gasp: 'My heart – the shock. Soon be better.'

Gradually the breathing eased. The colour returned and she opened her eyes. 'Brandy,' she whispered. 'For you too. And Caroline. I'll take it in.'

I fetched the brandy and glasses and after that Mrs Dring took charge. She gulped hers down and then told me to go and put iodine and plaster on my finger while she went to see to Caroline. I did this, and then returned to the hall and sat on the stool by the telephone until she came to tell me what to do next. I was capable of movement, even capable of reasoning, but all the springs of decision and of action had gone and the voice was still banging away at the back of my mind: kill a cripple, kill a crippled sister.

I began to think about my parents. How late would my

father come home? Had my mother already left the Clinic? I hoped Mrs Dring would remember them too and tell me what I ought to do. I didn't doubt her word that Caroline was all right but I was not conscious of any great relief. It didn't seem to make much difference. I'd murderously attacked her, with no thought of mercy as when I wrung the sparrow's neck, but with the will to terrify and hurt. And I'd tortured her first, slowly and deliberately, as she had the sparrow. There had been a good reason for it at the time but just now it didn't seem to matter. What I had done, I had done, and it was loathsome.

At last Mrs Dring returned. 'She's better,' she said. 'Swallowed the brandy all right and even said something. Reckon she'll have a very sore neck for a day or two though.'

'What did she say?' I asked.

'Couldn't rightly hear. Might've been "thank you". Might've been something else. Now I'm going to bathe it and see if I can find something good for bruises and later on we'll see if she'll swallow some hot milk and aspirin and when the Doctor comes in he can give her something more if he sees fit. Have you done up your finger yet?' She picked up my hand and inspected it. The blood was already seeping through the plaster. 'H'm. That'll do for the present. Reckon the Doctor'd better take a look at you too.'

It was a commonplace little remark but it seemed to do something to quieten those relentless hammer blows within me. It was as if she was indeed mopping up the casualties after a dog-fight; it put things in a different perspective, put my sister and myself more on a level. I became aware of the throbbing pain in my hand and I began to be conscious of something approaching relief.

And of gratitude. I got up off the stool. 'Oh, Mrs Dring, if you hadn't come back just then —' I stopped, remembering something. 'Good Lord, you'll miss the christening.'

'I've done that already. My daughter-in-law'll be mad at me but trouble's trouble and don't wait for nobody to be christened.'

I put my arms round her and dropped my head forward until it rested upon her scanty brown hair. She patted at me awkwardly.

'There, there. It'll be all right. There's no great harm done. Only a sore throat and a sore finger. Nothing that won't mend. Reckon it's too late to go to the Clinic now or I'd've said that's where you ought to be – going to fetch your Mum.'

I let her go and looked at my watch. 'Ten to five. I might just make it.'

'Off you go then. Mind how you drive.'

At the door I turned back, struck now with a sudden suspicion.

'Mrs D.,' I said, 'you're not just humouring me, are you? You're quite sure Caroline really *is* all right? I mean you're not simply telling me so to get me out of the flat and give me a chance to get away if I really have —'

I couldn't say the next words although they'd been going on incessantly in my head.

Mrs Dring caught hold of my jacket and shook me slightly.

'Now just you listen to me, Mr Richard Duncan,' she said. 'I've been seventeen years with your folks. That's ever since you were little more than a toddler. I've seen you through good times and I've seen you through bad. Your Dad's a fine clever man and I'd do anything for your dear Mum, and I'm sorry for Caroline and I'm sorry for you. And I know what you feel about Miss Janet 'cos I feel just the same.' She paused for breath and then went on, panting slightly. 'But I don't hold with killing people – provocation or no – not if you was the King of England. And if I wasn't sure she's had nothing worse than a bad fright and will be as right as rain in a day or two then you'd not be going through that door now – you'd be standing here with the police inspector putting handcuffs on you, that you would!'

'I'm sorry,' I said, and once again I leaned forward and kissed the thinning hair.

'So take care of yourself.' She pushed me out of the flat. 'And don't go wandering about but come straight back home if your Mum's already left,' she called after me.

Of course my mother had left the Clinic and taken a taxi home. I hadn't really expected to find otherwise and I don't think Mrs Dring had either. She had only wanted me out of the flat so that she could cope with everything quietly in my absence. And I had only done the half-hour drive in order to calm myself and regain some sense of purpose and direction. I didn't even bother to try and find a space for the mini in the crowded forecourt but simply left it at the kerb, blocking the flow of traffic. When I ran down the steps after speaking to the receptionist I saw a policeman advancing on it. I covered the remaining ground in three great strides, jumped in and moved off. The little incident gave me a great sense of satisfaction, quite out of proportion to its importance, since it would only have meant a warning or a small fine had I been caught.

But it restored my normal functioning. Evading the traffic cop seemed to hold in it all the great flow of relief that I hadn't experienced at the moment when

Mrs Dring told me that Caroline was all right. I drove on, humming to myself, and taking great pleasure in sneaking the road space from bigger or slower vehicles. I was heading for the West End, which wasn't the way I ought to have been going, but I felt a strong need to be isolated and yet not alone. There was comfort in losing myself in the crowd, being jumbled up with thousands of people full of troubles of their own, who knew nothing of me and cared less.

Or perhaps I was simply putting off the moment when I would take the little red notebook from my pocket. I hadn't yet looked inside it. It seemed very important to find exactly the right place to stop and study it. Certainly not at home. For all Mrs Dring's efforts, the atmosphere there would be more tense and heavy than ever. I didn't actually phrase it to myself that if I didn't go back yet then my parents would worry so much that when I did turn up their relief would outweigh their reproaches, but the idea must have been there all the same.

I'd got into the traffic milling round Hyde Park Corner by now and suddenly I was sick of it and didn't want to go any farther. I squeezed the mini in between two big American cars, noted with satisfaction that this was going to make it practically impossible for them to move, and walked into the park. For once there was sunshine; only intermittent, with plenty of black clouds rolling up between times, but when it did emerge it came in full glory, and the grass and the trees in their early summer green, and the sparkling water of the Serpentine and the dogs running and people strolling all combined to produce again that sense of elation that I had felt when driving off from the Clinic.

It was very strange, considering what had happened earlier, and considering what I felt about Janet and that I didn't even know if she was alive or dead. But youth is resilient, as the middle-aged so complacently say, and it makes one sick to hear it when one knows that everything is hopeless; but all the same, one can't be miserable every single moment of the time, and so I caught up with an Alsatian who seemed to have mislaid his owner, pulled the stick from his mouth, flung it ahead and then raced him to retrieve it, and finally came to a halt under a weeping willow tree at the side of the water, and it was there that I lay flat out on the grass and opened the notebook that contained Janet's diary.

It was written in her neat shorthand with the pages well filled and the symbols evenly spaced. It took me a little while to get the hang of it and, for all I had learnt, I wasn't able to make out every word. Often I wished I had the instruction book with me to refer to and sometimes I had to go back over a page several times to get the sense of it. But the more I read the easier it became and I don't think I ever went seriously wrong.

It started off on the Sunday in the middle of my Finals – the day when I had spent the afternoon and evening with Lesley, but it referred not only to the events of that day but to those of several weeks before. The sun disappeared behind a cloud as I began. It came out again later, but my upsurge of life and energy had gone and I lay with a heavy heart as the shadows lengthened on the grass and the little kids were collected by their mothers and taken home, and this is what I read:

Sunday, June 6

'I'm sure Caroline is trying to kill me. I feel better now that I've written it down in black and white, even if it's only in shorthand. There's nobody I can talk to. None of them, not even Richard, really knows what she's like and anyway it's not the sort of thing you can say about people to their relatives. I've tried to drop a hint to Matron and Sister Goodchild when they've asked me how I like living at the Duncans and they've been very kind but they don't really understand what it's like. They only know it through Uncle Andrew and all they say is that of course one has to be kind and patient living with a disabled person but that one must be a little tough too and make sure one lives one's own life. And I can't write to anyone back home. They wouldn't understand the situation here at all. They'd either say I was imagining it or tell me to go to the police. But how can I go to the police when it's my own cousin and her parents have been so kind to me and it's the only home I've got?

'Perhaps I am imagining it. I've gone over and over it in my mind until I feel as if I am going mad, but I'm going to write it all down now and try and see it a bit more clearly. It's risky to put anything on paper but if I write in this little notebook and always keep it in my handbag no one else will ever know about it and if anyone did find it they couldn't read shorthand. Except Richard perhaps, but I've just got to risk that. It wouldn't matter quite so much if he got hold of it as if one of the others did although I'm afraid he'd be very angry with me because after all Caroline is his sister.

'What I can't make out is whether she hates me because she thinks I'm taking him away from her or whether she just hates me because I can lead a normal life. Perhaps it's a bit of both. But she just loved telling me he was out with his best girl all today – simply loved it. I don't think I showed what I felt and I think that made her mad, that she couldn't make me jealous, and maybe that's why she did that frightful thing this afternoon – but I'd better not think about that just yet, I'd better think about the first time which was about two weeks ago.

'I don't see how I could have suspected anything. She asked me to put a new electric light bulb in her room. She said it wasn't bright enough and she wanted a 200-watt one for when she worked late at her studies in the evening. I did think she might have mentioned it when either Richard or Uncle Andrew was at home because they could have reached it easily by standing on a chair but I had to get the steps because the ceiling is so high. And Aunt Phyl had gone next door to see Mrs Anderson so she wasn't in the flat either.

'Caroline drove her wheelchair at the steps on purpose. I swear she did. They are rather old and unsteady and I'd have come a terrible crash if I hadn't happened to look down at that moment and been able to jump clear. I don't know how I managed it. And I caught hold of the stepladder too so that it didn't fall on her. But she only laughed.

'"Gosh, Janet, what a leap! Like a ballet dancer. I'm frightfully sorry. My hand slipped."

'It didn't. She manages her chair perfectly. She deliberately ran it at the wobbly back of the steps. I asked her if she was all right. I was shaking all over and terrified that she'd been hurt and that Uncle Andrew and Aunt Phyl would blame me for it. Suppose her back had been injured or she'd lost the use of her arms as well as her legs! It doesn't bear thinking of. And I did wonder whether perhaps I hadn't set the stepladder properly. "Don't tell Mummy or Daddy," she said. "They'll only worry." I promised not to. I put the steps back in the hall cupboard. I wasn't going to have another shot – not after that. Anyway she'd got her bedside lamp.

'"I'm awfully sorry, Janet," she said in that suffering

little voice of hers, "I do feel mean giving you such a fright when you are always so sweet and patient with your poor crippled cousin." What can one say to that? She knows it makes you feel so wretched that you only want to run away. "All the pleasures you give up because of me," she went on. "No dancing or boy friends. So sweet and unselfish. There aren't many people who would do that. Particularly with a most eligible young man right here in the very house."

'She went on like that for some time, rubbing in about that awful evening with Richard when Brian was staying with us. I suppose he meant it well really but oh dear I do wish he hadn't made me go out that time because she's been worse than ever since then. All the same I couldn't believe she was actually trying to hurt me. Not until this afternoon. But now I'm sure.

'I felt ever so much better last night when I found Richard had come home and I was hoping he'd be in all today, studying for his next week's exams. But I suppose it's more interesting to be with girls who know all about his studies than to be with someone who doesn't know anything like me so I can't blame him and I must try not to think about him so much. Anyway it was Caroline who persuaded Aunt Phyl to go for a drive with Uncle Andrew and I'd hoped when it was first suggested that Caroline would go too so that I could have the flat to myself which I rather like sometimes as it's less of a strain. She said she was too tired, though, and then Uncle Andrew and Aunt Phyl looked at me and I knew they wanted me to stay and look after Caroline because they get so little chance to do anything together, so of course I had to say that I would. I didn't like it but I'd made myself believe by then that the stepladder time was really an accident and in any case it sounded harmless enough when she came to my room after they had gone out and told me that the bathroom was rather mucky and she was afraid it was her fault because she'd just been using the toilet there. She always has to use that one because it's too awkward to get her chair into the one off the hall.

'I felt sorry for her. I knew she was vicious and hated me and I still felt sorry for her. It's so beastly to think she can only just manage to go to the toilet by herself. I can't help thinking about it and what an effort it must be pulling herself up out of the chair and clinging to the side of the washbasin and falling back on the lavatory seat and then all over again.

'I suppose it's better than not being able to manage at all but I should think it must make you feel you hate everybody and everything. So I felt sorry for her and I said of course I would go and clean up in the bathroom. Actually I didn't want to go at all. I don't mind the cleaning but I've got a stupid thing about using the bathroom. It's because there's nothing outside the window but a sheer drop down to the edge of the canal. You wouldn't think the back would be like that when there's such a posh-looking frontage to these flats but a lot of them round here seem to be like that – all show in front and dirty canals or railway embankments behind.

'It's so silly that it makes me ashamed even when I write it but I always feel I might somehow get shut in the bathroom and not able to get out. I like best to have my bath when I'm alone in the flat and can prop the door open but that doesn't often happen and the next best is when Aunt Phyl is doing something in the kitchen which is next door, and I feel safer because if I called out she would hear me. I don't think anyone has noticed this, nor that I always use the toilet in the front of the flat, which is quite natural because it's next to my room.

'I've always rather disliked small shut-in places but it never used to worry me like this – only since the crash. I suppose it must be because I was stuck in the back of the car all that time. Uncle Andrew would say that I was subconsciously aware of it even though I can't actually remember anything clearly. In fact I ought to tell Uncle Andrew because it's only an illness like any other and some of the patients are like that and they are treated and get better. But I still can't help feeling ashamed and in any case if I told Uncle Andrew then Caroline would get to know and I'd be absolutely terrified all the time if Caroline once got to know.

'But she doesn't know, thank goodness, and it was something quite different she had in mind when she asked me to clean up in the bathroom. There didn't seem to be anything much wrong when I looked in so I supposed she meant would I wash out the lavatory pan. I couldn't see the cleaner – there's usually some standing on the window-sill – so I supposed it must have run out and I went to the kitchen and got a bottle from the cupboard and then went back to the bathroom and left the door open with the stool against it. And I think it was that that saved me. The lid of the pan was down and so was the seat and I lifted them both up and poured a whole lot of the powder in and was going to pick up the brush to swish it around when suddenly it was like being banged over the head. I was sick and giddy all of a sudden. It was awful. Like the crash all over again.

'I got to the door by crawling and stayed there a while, trying not to vomit. I don't know where Caroline was. Perhaps she was listening round the corner of the passage or from behind her bedroom door but I didn't hear her at all. When I felt better I knew it wasn't just my nerves and that something had really made me ill and the last thing I had done was pour powder into the lavatory bowl. I got up somehow and pushed up the sash of the window to get more air and then I banged down the seat and collapsed on it. I was leaning forwards because I still felt frightfully sick and my arm was dragging on the floor and suddenly it touched something right behind the pan and I got hold of it and pulled it out.

'It was a bottle of liquid cleaner with some of it used. I read the label – "Not to be used with any other cleaner" – and then I knew. There must have been some of it in the bowl when I poured the powder in and it gives off a poisonous gas. We don't usually have the liquid cleaner but it looked as if this had been a free sample. Caroline must have put it in after the others went out and then tricked me into pouring the powder on top. It's so horrible that I can hardly believe it but that's what must have happened. I thought at first that I'd go and accuse her, but it wouldn't have been any use because she'd only have asked how on earth *she* could push a bottle right down at the back of the W.C. – and in fact she must have had quite a job doing it – and she'd have said it must have been Aunt Phyl or Mrs Dring left the liquid in the bowl and that she hadn't meant me to clean that out but only to wipe the floor where she'd splashed from the wash-basin.

'I didn't see how I could prove anything so I just flushed it all away and put both cleaners on the window-sill where everyone could see them and went and lay on my bed till I felt better. Caroline must have been in her room and I didn't see her till evening. And I told them I was tired and was going to bed early.

'I've been writing a long time. I'd better put the light

out now and try and sleep. It sounds as if they've gone to bed but I haven't heard Richard come in yet. I suppose he's enjoying himself too much, if he really has gone out with this girl. I think I'd better try to stop thinking about that.'

Monday, June 7

'I haven't seen Richard at all today. I hope he liked his papers. I am terribly unhappy about Aunt Phyl. I had no idea she was so ill. She never complains. I'm glad they told me in a way but it'll be difficult not saying anything to Richard or Caroline. I can see they don't want him to worry while he's doing his exams but I think they ought to tell Caroline. I think she suspects something and is frightened and that makes her worse than ever to me.

'I don't think now that she actually wants me dead but I think she would like me to be hurt and perhaps be a cripple like herself. When we have talked about the accident and me having concussion and ribs broken I've had an idea she's been angry because I got better and that if I'd come here limping for life she'd probably have been nice to me. I know that's what Richard thinks.

'It seems awful to keep on thinking about oneself like this all the time when poor Aunt Phyl is so worried. After all there's nothing really that Caroline can do to me. She's very helpless and I'm all right now and what I've got to do is keep a very close watch on her and avoid being tricked again.'

Tuesday, June 8

'I've got to be alone with Caroline in the flat again and I'm so afraid but I don't see how to avoid it. Uncle Andrew asked me as a particular favour. He's taking Aunt Phyl to another specialist on Thursday afternoon

to get a second opinion and they don't want to leave
Caroline alone for so long. So I'm to come home for the
afternoon and they'll be back as soon as they can but it
may be quite late. I wish I could think of an excuse. I
can't think of anything. Matron doesn't mind. And of
course they've no idea I'm so frightened of Caroline.
They know she's bitchy to me sometimes but then so
she is to everybody. I can't tell just now when they
are so worried. I can't. I can't. And I've got to pretend to
Caroline about where they are, too. I must get through
the afternoon somehow. It's only for a few hours. I'll do
some cooking. That'll take my mind off it a bit. Make
some cakes that Caroline will like. She's awfully greedy.
I suppose it's having so few other pleasures. Surely she
can't be so bad to me if I'm actually making cakes for her.
And some for Richard too. It's his last exam. If only he
has done all right. I don't believe he is no good, as he says.
I'm sure they are all very clever indeed. I'm sure he's as
good as Caroline any day. Only he does worry so much
about what his father thinks of him. I suppose I would too
if I had a father like Uncle Andrew.

'All the same I've decided to tell Uncle Andrew about
this awful feeling of being afraid to be shut in. As soon as
he's less worried about Aunt Phyl. It's stupid to go on
like this because it's really only an illness that can be
cured and Uncle Andrew can send me to one of the
other doctors at the hospital if he doesn't think he ought
to treat me himself. And as soon as Richard has finished
his exams I'm going to tell him about Caroline. I don't
think he will say I'm imagining it and I think he may be
able to stop her because she's a bit frightened of him.

'Only I mustn't let him suspect anything till after his
exams. I've got to get through Thursday afternoon
somehow.'

                                             Wednesday, June 9

'It's coming very near now, tomorrow afternoon, and it was terribly difficult to behave as usual this evening. It's lovely to see Richard happy again. I'm sure he's done all right. This time tomorrow and it will all be over. For him and for me. I wonder what he'd think if he knew what I was writing now? I wonder what he really does think about me? I really did think for one moment that perhaps he ... but there are all those clever girls at college, and Caroline says – and I'm sure Uncle Andrew wouldn't approve and anyway it's not supposed to be a good thing – first cousins —

'I wonder whether there is any chance for me at all.'

9

I PUT the notebook down on the grass and rubbed my eyes. I had been reading for a long time. The sun was sinking now, giving colour to the tree trunks and the water. There were fewer people about and there was a slight chill in the air, although we were well on in June. I picked up the book again, sick with apprehension, cursing these stupid hieroglyphics that made my progress so slow.

There weren't many more written pages now. There was no date to the last entry. The neat symbols and even margins had come to an end and instead there were long untidy marks scrawled right across the page – some scarcely recognisable as shorthand outlines, and much even written in sprawling longhand. It had been written under intense emotion and stress. I read with my heart racing and my mind in tumult, turning each page before I'd fully made out the previous one, going back again, repeating the words aloud as I deciphered them, and in between whiles exclaiming aloud to myself.

'Oh God what shall I do – she's done it – she's locked me in – oh God help me God help me – if I write perhaps I'll keep calm – just keep on writing keep on writing – I've got my book here – always with me in my bag and pencil too – if I write it all and try not to think then I'll keep steady keep down the panic and someone will come and let me out – she asked me to get her pills from the bathroom medicine cupboard she said she hadn't any more in her room and her pain was bad and I couldn't say no – she was groaning in pain – and I saw the key wasn't in the bathroom door as it should be and I didn't like it but I couldn't say no and I thought I'd be in and out in a flash and she was waiting in the corridor and I thought she couldn't possibly get here and do anything before I got out, but the pills weren't on the bottom shelf and I had to push bottles aside before I could see and she was just outside groaning in pain and I couldn't find the bottle and I had to get the stool to reach the top shelf and then I knew what she was doing behind my back and I was so in panic I slipped off the stool and hit my leg and it slowed me up and she'd pulled the door shut and I got to the handle and I pulled and pulled again but it didn't open so I knew she was pulling the other side and her hands are strong and mine were shaking and I knew she was going to turn the key and God help me I'm locked in I can't get out and it's getting worse – I can't breathe – I can't get out – it's closing in – getting darker and darker – nearer and nearer – it's crushing me – it's dark – I can't see I can't breathe —

'It's eased a bit. I got a bottle and swallowed a sedative pill and if it only works it might keep me calm and someone will come soon and let me out. I thought perhaps I could find something to turn the key from inside or push it out and get it from under the door but she's taken it away – she's gone away, I called to her to let me out but she'd gone away.

'What else can I do – I can't break the door it's too solid – no glass and I shouted out of the window but there's no one to hear, there's only the canal and they wouldn't hear from above unless they look out as it's only bathroom windows —

'I shouted and shouted and nobody hears and I looked down and it's a long way down and there's a narrow bit of gravel and then the water – if a barge came along they'd see me but there aren't any barges there's nothing but walls and water and 1 can't shout more my voice is paralysed – paralysed and that drug isn't helping – it's making it worse – it's coming back – it's worse than ever – it's closing in – I can't breathe – I can't see – I'm going mad - it's screaming and screaming - it's coming at me – I'm going mad – I must get out – I can't move – I can't see can't breathe get out get out get out. . . .'

I put the book back in my pocket and I held my hands over my face. Her screams seemed to be ringing in my ears. The car crash had been at night – in the dark. And her head had received a blinding blow, and her ribs had been crushed, and help had been long in coming and longer still before they cut her out.

I got to my feet and walked slowly and unsteadily across the grass. My hands were clenching and unclenching. If I'd had Caroline there 1 would have wrung her neck without a qualm. The canal. They'd have to drag the canal. If we had known at once! If it had only just happened when I got home there'd have been a chance. She might have swum a bit. I might have saved her. But drowning doesn't take long, and in her state of shock, and in that filthy water. . . .

Suddenly I began to run, assailed by a sense of great urgency. But what could I do, what did minutes or even hours matter after all this time? My fingers kept up their twisting motion. It was murder, particularly vicious and cruel murder. And in a flash of memory there came to me a fragment of a television show, an idle remark of Caroline's: the plot was to play upon a woman's fears until she killed herself.

Not such an idle remark. Murder premeditated, murder planned from the very first.

I reached the car and found there occupation for my restless hands. They worked automatically. I made my way homewards without conscious decision. I knew only one thing. This was murder and there was justice to be done. Not by me, but by the law. No wonder Caroline had been so hysterical when I came home that fatal day. She had opened the bathroom door and found Janet gone, the window open. It had worked perfectly, and she had all the clearing up to do. She must have thought quickly and moved slowly and agonisingly. Someone might come in any minute; her state of mind must have been terrible. What had she done? Picked up the notebook, looked inside it, been unable to resist taking it away to try and read it. And the handbag. Thrown it out of the window most likely, and then shut down the sash. That must have been some struggle – getting her chair in position, propping herself against the washbasin. She would have had to fumble and strain and fail and then strain and strain again.

Perhaps she hadn't managed to get the window right down. Perhaps she had thrown the handbag down the rubbish shute. If only we had known at the time! It was much too late to find any clues now. Except that clues no longer mattered because it was all down in Janet's diary and Caroline was going to have to tell the truth. No amount of pathos and ingenuity and sickness feigned or real was going to get her out of the evidence that was tucked in my pocket.

It was nearly dark now. I'd been gone for several hours. For the first time I began to think of my parents – the shock when they came home to find I'd attacked Caroline, the not knowing where I was. They would have worse shocks still to follow, when they learned what I had to tell.

Perhaps it was because I wanted to put off the evil moment; perhaps it was because I had a longing to look upon Janet's ghastly grave, or perhaps there was some other motive, but for whatever reason, I found myself slowing down as I came the last half-mile between the acres of derelict land and when I got to the canal I pulled the mini half up on to the kerb and got out to lean on the parapet. Maybe that dark water would tell me something; maybe from somewhere she would speak to me.

I was so absorbed in my thoughts and feelings that at first I was unaware of the commotion going on only a few yards away. It came nearer and I could ignore it no longer. It was a group of youths – not hippy-types but boys from the new estate – and they were occupied in a violent punch-up. My first instinct was to leg it back to the car and join the few other passing motorists who were keeping carefully out of their way. If conscience pricked, I could phone the police from the box at the next corner or after I got home. And then I saw more clearly what the fight involved. It was no evenly balanced gang war; it looked like three to one. And the three were the bigger and the one was losing badly. They'd got him pinned against the parapet; they really were going to crucify him.

I'm often accused of being impulsive and it riles me and I always deny it, but sometimes I can see what people mean. I don't remember thinking about anything at all until I was right in the middle of it. I had the great advantage of taking them by surprise and I'd aimed a near knockout blow at the biggest of them and sent the next biggest one staggering before they realised what was happening and turned on me. And after that I began to take it all until the little one recovered himself and tried to do his stuff.

We were the losing side, though. I got in some good bashes but I was receiving far more, and after a while they had me down and my head hit the wall and the world turned upside down. Some public-spirited passer-by must have done something about it by then, because I came back to life to find a couple of blue uniforms standing over me and no sign of the gang. They helped me to my feet. I staggered, stamped on the pavement, experimented with movements.

'Are you all right?' one of them asked, but without much sympathy.

'Basically, yes,' I replied. 'At least I think so. There's a certain amount of superficial damage but nothing serious I believe.'

They looked taken aback at my words and my accent; they must have supposed me to be one of the gang. Clothes are meaningless but upbringing and education still give one an advantage that nothing can take away – nothing in our class-conscious society, that is. It's very wrong but sometimes it's very useful too. I told them who I was and all about it and they obviously thought I was quite mad but they didn't disbelieve a word. They wanted to take me to a hospital but I persuaded them that I only needed some domestic first aid. They wouldn't let me drive, however, but one of them got into the mini and I sat in the panda car with the other.

Actually I was glad of their help. My head was throbbing and I was aching all over. And the plaster had come off the finger that Caroline had bitten and I was dripping blood from that and other cuts. It wasn't fair to appear suddenly in front of my parents looking like this and I thought that it would be a good idea if one of the policemen went in first to explain. The one who was driving me agreed to do this.

'You can clean up a bit and I'll wait to take your statement,' he added. And then a moment or two later he exclaimed in surprise. 'We won't be needed. There's the Inspector's car.'

It was parked outside our block. I felt pleased because it meant I could tell him at once about Janet and no time would be lost in searching the canal. But I felt very impatient waiting in the panda car while the news of my beating-up was broken to my parents and after a minute of it I could bear it no longer and I rushed in.

They were standing in the hall – all of them, my father and my mother and Inspector Soames and the police driver, and the latter seemed to be about half-way through his story.

'Don't worry about me,' I cried. 'I'm all right. I'll tell you later. Inspector – I know what happened – to Janet I mean. She got shut in the bathroom. She's got claustrophobia badly. She panicked and tried to get out – she jumped out of the window —'

They looked at me with mingled amazement, horror, incredulity. Inspector Soames spoke, humouring me. 'Right. You can tell me all about that in a moment and about this punch-up too. But the most important thing now is to —'

I interrupted him. 'You don't believe me?' I looked round the circle of faces. I must have looked very wild. 'It's true! It's written down – she kept a diary – she carried it with her always. It's in shorthand but I can read it.' I was fumbling in my jacket pocket. I was shaking and my head was bursting and I was very near collapse. 'I put it here!' I cried.

My fingers dug deeper. I tried the other pockets. There was nothing in any of them. My wallet was gone, my pen, all loose change. And the red notebook too.

'They robbed me!' I cried. 'When they knocked me out. But the money's nothing. It's the book. I've got to go back – I've got to find it!'

I made for the door. Two of them got hold of me – my father and the Inspector. The police driver stood in front of the door. The Inspector's steady tones penetrated the fog around me.

'Take it easy now. One of us will go. Just tell us what it looked like.'

'A little red memo book – from Woolworths,' I gasped. 'Half-full of shorthand. But I've got to go. I've *got* to!'

I tried to fight them off. My mother came forward.

'Please, Richard,' she said in a low voice, 'let the police search. They'll find it if it is to be found. Please don't try to go out again. You've had enough. *We*'ve had enough.'

I ceased struggling. And there was something in the way she spoke that made me ask:

'Caroline? You know about —?'

'Yes, we know. She's all right. She can't talk much but she told us. She's very ashamed. She admitted she was tormenting you by pretending she knew some nasty things about Janet. She says it was nearly all her fault, that she went too far.'

I sat down on the hall stool. My head was whirling. So that was to be the line. I thought she was done for but she'd got one more wriggle left. She'd take all the blame for my assault on her in return for my silence about the diary. I could think no more. I must have groaned aloud. My father got me by the arm and pulled me upright.

'Come along now and we'll attend to these cuts. Can't you see it's distressing your mother?'

I must indeed have looked an awful bloody sight. I let myself be guided along the corridor. At the door of the bathroom I stopped.

'I can manage on my own,' I said.

'Possibly,' replied my father. 'I'd like to have a look at you all the same.'

I submitted with a bad grace. As he was removing encrusted blood from round my eye he said with a bitterness that I could not fail to notice:

'I suppose you think me incapable even of dressing a wound.'

I was taken aback. It's odd how one sometimes manages to forget that Dad really is a doctor. I didn't know what to reply.

'I was doing my stint on the casualty wards years before you were born,' he went on.

I still couldn't think of anything to say. I could feel myself wincing and it wasn't from the pain of antiseptics. The next remark was spoken so softly that I barely caught the words.

'Perhaps that's where I ought to have stayed. Perhaps this is all I'm fit for.'

I couldn't help squirming. I moved my head abruptly and his hand brushed painfully against my injured eye. 'Ouch!' I yelled loudly, in order to relieve my feelings.

'Keep still, can't you,' he snapped.

'I'm sorry,' I muttered. And then a moment later. 'I'm sorry to be such a bloody nuisance. Getting beaten-up, I mean.'

He didn't answer for a minute or two. We'd got down to my right hand by then. Caroline's effort stood out clearly among the bruises resulting from contact with jawbone and muscle. My father studied it for a moment and then he said:

'Don't do it again. You've paid your debt.'

'What d'you mean?' I asked.

'You used your strength to attack a helpless creature. You had to ease your guilt by going to the rescue of another helpless creature. All right. That's enough now. You've made expiation. You've punished yourself enough.'

'Oh.' I still stared stupidly. 'Is that what I've been doing?'

'Well, what's your own opinion? Do you usually make a practice of taking part in gang warfare?'

'No,' I admitted, 'but I might still have crashed in on this one. I'd have phoned for the police first, though.'

'Exactly. Good citizenship, not masochism.'

'Oh.' I chewed over this while the rest of the dressings were being done. It seemed to make sense and it also made me feel a little better to think of it that way. But I still wished he hadn't opened that little window on to his own self-reproach, because I couldn't help but think it justified and I couldn't help blaming him for what Caroline had become.

When he had finished he stood back and surveyed me and said:

'That's about the lot. You're lucky it was no worse. They might have had knives. You've got off very lightly. Taking on three at once. Ridiculous.'

'Oh well.' I stood up and helped stow away the first-aid kit. 'You know how it is – fools rush in —'

He was washing his hands and seemed not to hear me. 'All the same,' he murmured as if to himself, 'I'm glad you did join in that fight.' And then he added, again so low as to be almost inaudible: 'It makes up a bit for – it makes it seem worth while after all.'

• • • • •

After that conversation I simply couldn't face telling my father what I had found out about Caroline, nor telling my mother either. I lay awake most of the night wondering what to do and trying to find a position that didn't make my aches and bruises feel worse than ever. Eventually I fell asleep on the decision to go and see Inspector Soames first thing in the morning. I hadn't any hope that Janet's diary would be found, but I did think the Inspector would give me a fair hearing. He and my father had become quite friendly during the course of the enquiries about Janet and he seemed a thoughtful sort of person who could understand a family set-up such as ours.

It was very convenient that I had to go to the police station to make a statement about the fight, but I didn't tell them at home that I was going to talk about Janet too. Caroline was being kept in bed and in any case it was just as well for me to keep away from her. My father was seeing some patients at home that morning, and my mother was occupied with Mrs Dring. It all felt sur-prisingly normal, very much as it had been in the days before Janet came to live with us, and this offended me, because it gave me the feeling that nobody cared any longer what had happened to her except myself.

I spent some time in the bathroom before I went out. Mrs Dring had just finished her scrubbing and it all looked very clean and hygienic and harmless. I sat on the edge of the bath and tried to imagine Janet in her in-creasing panic. It isn't easy to think oneself into somebody else's phobia and all I could think of was that if I got shut in there by mistake I would probably have a leisurely bath to pass the time and then, if still not released, take down the first-aid manual that lived up on the corner of the cupboard and brush up my knowledge. But of course

I hadn't been recently trapped in a car in a bad road accident.

When I started thinking about that I did begin to feel something of what Janet must have gone through and I remembered how shaken she had been that evening when Caroline insisted on talking of the experience. If only she had told someone at once instead of battling on like that! But of course one doesn't tell people about one's secret fears; apart from anything else, it gives them such a hold over you. Especially somebody like Caroline.

Caroline must have guessed it that very first evening and been waiting her chance all along. There is a bolt inside the bathroom door and the key is quite unnecessary, but just happens to be left there, presumably on the inside of the door, but I can't say I've ever taken much notice of it. Caroline must have had her chair stationed right outside the door when she was groaning for her pills, with the key held ready out of sight, waiting until Janet was occupied at the cupboard. I wondered where she had been during Janet's frantic bangings and cryings – for I felt sure the scrawled entries in the notebook must have been interspersed with much more desperate and uncontrolled activity.

I inspected the window. One could easily stand on the edge of the bath and swing oneself up to sit gripping the sash, with legs dangling outwards. To get into a position for taking a leap big enough to clear the path and carry one into the water was a little more difficult. She'd have had to stand outside on the sill gripping the sash like a window cleaner. I swung myself up and experimented. I was battered and sore from last night's fight but I could manage it comfortably. I hung on and looked around. There was no one to be seen. Only the backs of the buildings our side of the canal and the hoardings skirting the railway land on the other. Unless someone actually happened to be leaning out of a bathroom window like ours at the vital moment it would be perfectly possible, even in broad daylight, to take such a leap without anybody being any the wiser.

I felt very inclined to try it, to see whether the splash would arouse any interest and to see how it felt to swim in that foul water. It smelt repulsive too, but it wasn't that so much that put me off as much as the thought of having to come home covered with scum and oil and perhaps run into one of the patients and in any case give my poor mother another shock. In the end I decided it would be best to leave the experimenting until after I'd seen the Inspector and had got his authority to back me up.

I had to wait some time at the police station before he was free, but apparently I was in good favour there for having launched out at what appeared to be quite a well-known little group of thugs and we were having a lively discussion about boxing in general when I was sent for.

The Inspector listened very patiently to my somewhat confused story. It was long and complicated and I kept having to interrupt myself to go back to an important point that I had forgotten, and there was also the problem of constantly switching about from my own experience of events at the time to the version I had learnt from Janet's diary. When I finished he continued doodling on his blotter and said, without looking up:

'Your sister is a very sick girl.'

'I know.'

'She suffers in her mind, too, as well as being paralysed.'

'I know that as well.'

I began to feel a rising tension. I had a horrible

suspicion that he was going to tell me that I must be particularly patient and understanding because I was tough and healthy. But he didn't. He simply sighed heavily and said:

'It's very difficult.'

'But there's no need to bring my parents in, is there?' I asked. 'I'm sure I didn't mention Caroline last night – I'm sure I only said that Janet got locked in. They can think she got the key stuck or something —'

'Perhaps she did,' said the Inspector quietly.

'But – but —'

'It's not impossible in a case of severe phobia. The mind is temporarily so unhinged that the subject sometimes acts in such a way to bring about the very circumstances he is dreading. Your father would be able to explain that to you.'

Again I had to bite back my impatience. The Inspector seemed to have acquired such a deference for my father that it looked as if he wasn't going to be any help at all. I didn't want any more psychological theories; I wanted action.

'But Caroline had the key!' I cried.

'That may be just an assumption. As far as I recollect from *your* recollection of the diary – and it is a pity that you lost it I must say – Miss Packington stated that she pulled at the handle and it wouldn't open and she knew that your sister had locked the door from the outside. Now I don't doubt for one moment that Miss Packington suffered from very severe claustrophobia. But it is not inconceivable that in the intensity of her panic she imagined the door to be locked when in fact it wasn't. It might have swung shut of its own accord or in a slight draught from the open window – it's a heavy old door as I remember from my tour of your flat at the time and this could well have happened. Or Miss Packington might have tugged at it without fully turning the handle, which I believe is on the stiff side, and her own fears created the rest. I don't suppose you would ever have been interested in reading any of Jane Austen's novels, but in fact there is a delightfully ironic episode in *Northanger Abbey* when a very young girl, in the vividness of her imagined horrors, believes a cabinet to be locked and unopenable when all the time it was she who had turned the key and locked it in the first place.'

'But the diary,' I said. 'Those last entries.'

'That wouldn't invalidate them.'

'And Caroline – if that's what happened why didn't she call out to Janet that it was all right? Why didn't she open the door herself? Why did she go away? Why did she send Janet in for her pills in the first place?'

'Perhaps because she was in pain and really wanted her pills,' was the Inspector's quiet reply. 'Perhaps the pain was so bad that she was not capable of taking any action at all during the next few moments. Perhaps when she was able to move her chair she went away because she didn't want anyone to see her in her extremity.'

I remembered Caroline's hysteria when I arrived home that day. All along I had believed that to be genuine enough. My brain was beginning to reel.

'But she must have gone to the bathroom later,' I protested, 'because she *had* got the diary – and the handbag was gone and the window was down.'

'That is undeniable. We might however suppose that she was able to guess what had happened and was so alarmed at the thought that she might come under suspicion that she took what protective action she could.'

In all my confusion I was yet conscious of irritation

that the Inspector should so obviously be trying to talk like my father.

'And what about the other attempts then – the knocking against the stepladder, the trick with the lavatory cleaners?'

'It is difficult to know what to think of that,' the Inspector said after a short pause. 'With regard to the first incident I would say that we must remember your sister is very proud. Such movement as she is capable of she performs competently and well. I believe it is immensely painful to her that her awkwardness has to be observed by others all the time. I think she might find it more tolerable to be suspected of evil intent than to be suspected of clumsiness with her hands too.'

I stared at him in astonishment. I wanted to protest again, but my reason told me that he could be right.

'As to the lavatory cleaner,' he went on, 'there could be many explanations. Your sister may well have poured some into the bowl, leaving Miss Packington to do the more strenuous part of the job. The bottle might then have fallen on the floor and rolled away out of her reach. I don't know why it should have occurred to her to mention it nor to give a warning against using the powder. I believe Miss Packington was in the habit of performing little domestic tasks from time to time. She might be assumed to be competent in this respect.'

It was as if a revolving stage was turning in front of my eyes. The scene I had had such a clear view of was disappearing and a totally new picture was taking its place. But it was too much to take in all at once.

'But Janet's a sensible girl,' I said. 'She's a kind-hearted, sensitive, sympathetic sort of girl. She's not a pathological liar. She doesn't make up stories to accuse other people. If she says she was being attacked, then she was being.'

'We have no evidence,' said the Inspector. 'We have only the unspoken suspicions of a young girl still suffering considerably from the after-effects of severe concussion and double bereavement and possibly – if you'll excuse my mentioning it – from a certain amount of jealousy arising from the attachment which she appears to have formed to yourself.'

'But it's the other way round! It's Caroline who was so jealous of Janet!'

'I don't doubt it. It can work both ways, though.'

I leaned my head on my hands and groaned aloud. 'I suppose you think I've been making it all up. I suppose you think I'm lying. I suppose you think I'm potty too —'

'No, indeed,' he said. 'I believe you to be perfectly honest. And also perfectly normal, though living in a difficult situation and under considerable strain.'

'Blindly stupid, then.'

'Which of us isn't blind when it comes to our own affections and to women's machinations around us?'

I got to my feet and moved around the little office. 'I don't know what the hell to believe now,' I said . 'You've got me so muddled that I don't trust anything any more. You think they are both unbalanced then – both Caroline and Janet?'

'Up to a point, yes.'

'Caroline *did* resent her! She was always being bitchy to her. My parents know that. They'd bear that out.'

'Yes. That I certainly do believe.'

'But it didn't go as far as attempts at murder? Is that what you're trying to say?'

'I would certainly like a great deal more evidence before trying to reach a conclusion.'

'But what are we going to do?' I cried, stopping in front of the desk and leaning my hands on it. 'Whether

Caroline was responsible or not, we've got to find Janet.
We've got to. I don't care if she is a bit neurotic. She's all
I care for – all I ever will!'

He looked up at me bleakly and shook his head. 'Don't
be too hopeful,' he said. 'We can but do our best.'

'But now that you know what happened – the canal –
perhaps she got out – perhaps she did manage to swim —'

'Naturally we shall attend to the canal. But don't lose
sight of one more possibility.'

'What's that?'

'That she was able to open the door of the bathroom
after all. That she picked up her handbag and walked out
of the flat, forgetting about the notebook and leaving it
lying on the bathroom floor.'

We stared at each other and this time it was I who
continued to develop the theory.

'In that case,' I said, 'she might have pulled the window
down again. And when Caroline came in there would
only be the diary left. And Caroline might have been in
her room and not heard Janet go out. So that Caroline
really didn't know what had happened to Janet at all. So
that except for picking up the diary Caroline's story
might be true.' I stopped. I was rushing towards the
conclusion that I dreaded to reach. The Inspector waited
silently. I looked away and went on:

'And Caroline might have hidden the diary not
because she thought Janet might have accused her of
anything but because she hoped – because she hoped to
find out whether Janet and I —'.

I could say no more. I felt that I was choking.

'Exactly,' said the Inspector.

10

So long as I was with the Inspector I remained convinced that Caroline was innocent at least of any actual attack on Janet, but when I was on my way home the scene began to shift again. I remembered in particular that evening with the sparrow and I told myself that I had allowed myself to be over-persuaded by the speech for the defence and that I had been too ready to abandon my own deepest instinct about what had really happened. Anyway, how did Inspector Soames know so much about Caroline at all? It wasn't as if he was a close personal friend, only a recent acquaintance. He could have learned it only from one source; he had been brain-washed by my father to take Caroline's part.

As I thought this, resentment flared up again. Why didn't my father talk to me direct instead of sheltering behind a policeman? But anger soon ebbed away. I'd hardly given him a chance. I wasn't exactly easy to talk to. And in any case he knew nothing about the contents of Janet's diary. He only knew about Caroline's general beastliness and he was making no attempt to deny that nor to excuse himself from blame. On the contrary, in fact. If I were to go rushing to him now and tell him what Janet had written, which in my doubt and confusion on leaving the police station I had felt inclined to do, it was quite possible that he would take my part and sink even deeper into remorse and grief and self-abasement. And all to no purpose. It would make no difference to the search for Janet; it would help nobody, and it quite well might not even be true.

I turned aside when I was nearly home and once more

paused to lean over the canal. Presumably they would drag it now. But even the thought of that didn't bring much comfort. This was the spot where I had rushed in to do battle last night. How easy that had been! No question whose side to take, the issue absolutely clear. But to the battle now going on in my mind there was no simple solution. Did I or did I not believe my sister to be guilty of trying to drive to her death the girl whom I loved?

I'd got to sort it out, and quickly too. If I believed her guilty then I must leave home immediately, for to remain would be intolerable. And all my earlier efforts to help at home would have been in vain. And my mother with her illness still in the balance; and my father who in spite of all did seem to care what happened to me, and who had come off his lofty perch for one fleeting second last night and revealed that he'd have liked to join in the fight too and was glad I had done so because it made up to him for —

For what? For his heartbreak over Caroline, of course.

Round and round the arguments went. But I knew all this; had known it for ages. There was nothing different now. Except for Janet and for Caroline's guilt. Ever more desperately did I try to prove that Caroline was guilty, to force myself to remember every spiteful remark she had ever uttered, every little dig and thrust she had ever made at me. She *had* to have done it; she *had* to have laid booby traps for Janet to fall into; she *had* to have worked upon Janet's weakness in order to drive her temporarily out of her mind.

My head was throbbing badly. I was still weak from last night's activities.

'That's enough now. You've punished yourself quite enough.'

I could hear my father saying it in his normal voice, his steady, professional, quietly authoritative voice. And it was quite enough too. I didn't want any more. Neither blows nor stabs of conscience, nor doubts and uncertainties. I was sick of it all, and anyway it was no use struggling any longer. I felt in my heart that the Inspector could be right; that Janet's nervous fears had made of Caroline a greater monster than she was, that my love for Janet had joined me with them and, above all, that I was fighting this desperate rearguard action to prove Caroline's guilt in order to ward off the fresh waves of shame and self-loathing that would assail me when I thought again of my treatment of her.

There was no dodging them. I'd just got to face it. I'd been cruel and unjust and I'd simply have to try to make up for it now. It was part of life, like thugs at street corners and Mother's illness and losing someone the moment you began to care for her.

I turned away from the canal full of good resolves. And as I came up to our block I saw a patient of my father's coming out, a good-looking young man who had had a brilliant academic record and seemed all set for great achievements. But he was a hopeless schizophrenic and there was very little that could be done to cure him. I glanced round at him again and suddenly I felt a great upsurge of relief and gratitude and could have gone on my knees and thanked God if I'd believed there to be a God to thank. I might be rash and quick-tempered and sometimes obtuse and sometimes too easily swayed, but the fact remained that I was sound in mind and body and had all life ahead of me.

One has to find this sort of thankfulness out for oneself if one is really to feel it: it's no good other people trying to din it into you. But when it comes like this in a flood then it is a gift in itself, a blessing as great as those for which one is giving thanks. And it's when you feel this great warmth of gratitude right from the heart of you that you can at last detach yourself from your guilt and feel true pity.

So I believed that I had at last solved the problem of my attitude to my sister, and that henceforth I should see her in the clear-sighted way that the Inspector had done, and this would enable me to be kind. But big resolves are so easily upset by little irritations, and when I opened the front door my mother was dusting the hall and she shushed me because of the patients although in fact I hadn't made any noise at all; and then I said I was hungry and as lunch was to be late I'd go along to the kitchen and make myself a sandwich, and she got very agitated and said she'd bring me one along to the dining-room and I told her not to fuss so, making so much work for herself; and then it turned out that Caroline was up and having a little meal in the kitchen and that I was to be kept right away from Caroline, though Mother didn't put it in those words.

Of course I enquired sarcastically how it was proposed to carry out this policy, with both of us in the flat, and were we to have our meals in relays, and how long was I expected to remain on probation. At that point my mother began to cry, and Mrs Dring came along the corridor and put an arm round her and looked at me reproachfully. And then my father came out of the consulting-room to summon the next patient who was sitting in the waiting-room, and he glared at us for causing such a commotion, and indeed we were making rather a noise by then; and I said that obviously there was no place for me at home and I'd better go straight out again and get a sandwich in the coffee bar, which I did.

All very stupid and trivial, but it cured me of my grand resolutions and when I came back again for lunch, at which Caroline was not present, I was right back in the familiar old tangle of family relationships again.

After lunch I went and sat in Janet's room, trying to feel her presence, trying to re-create my image of her. But in spite of her little bits and pieces on the dressing-table and her clothes hanging in the wardrobe, I found it difficult to form a clear picture and I wished more than ever that I had not lost the diary. I should have liked to linger on those sentences where she referred to myself. But there was also all the part about Caroline and the terrible end. If only Inspector Soames had read it for himself, surely he would not so glibly have dismissed it all as accident, have come down so firmly on Caroline's side?

The ding-dong conflict began again. And only a short while ago I thought I had resolved it. It was the not knowing that was so intolerable. Almost worse than not knowing what had become of Janet, because I had very little hope that she wasn't dead. I sat on the edge of the divan bed, feeling every moment more depressed and looking back with something like nostalgia to the past few days when I had had the clue of the shorthand books to follow up and when all my thoughts and efforts were concentrated on how to drag the truth out of Caroline.

Of course I couldn't possibly try to talk to her again, but there was something else that I could do. I could put Janet's version and the Inspector's version to the test. My father had gone to the hospital and the others were resting. It was a favourable moment to go on with the experiments that I had started in the morning, with this fresh theory in mind to guide me now.

There was no key in the bathroom door and it was

propped open by the stool, letting some air through on this rather sultry day. I moved the stool aside with a quick gesture and was interested to see that the door immediately swung shut in the little breeze from the open window. Janet had had to use the stool to reach the medicine cupboard. Presumably it had been propping open the door, and this was what had happened when she moved it.

I grasped the doorhandle from the inside with my right hand and turned it carefully clockwise, which is the way one would normally open a door. Then I pulled, taking care not to make my movements too forceful, trying to judge the amount of effort that Janet would have put forth.

The door didn't budge at all and for just the split second before I realised what must have happened I felt an uncomfortable little sinking feeling and during that fraction of time I had a tiny glimpse of what it must be like to suffer from claustrophobia. Of course the solution was simple enough. The latch was faulty and didn't click back at all if you turned the handle that way. You had to turn it round anti-clockwise, right far round and keep it gripped there while you pulled, in order to open the door. I'd been using the bathroom all the time, as had the others, and I suppose we had noticed that the latch was slipping, but being very preoccupied, and having by experimenting found the way to overcome it, we had adjusted ourselves subconsciously to this minor inconvenience, as one does, and were scarcely aware of it because it was of no importance to us.

Even Caroline. But for Caroline the actual opening of the door was a very unimportant part of the elaborate and lengthy ritual of using the bathroom.

I shut the door again, once more turned the handle

clockwise, and pulled in vain. If this was your own particular horror and if the fear that someone was going to make it come true was stifling your reason and you were anyway in a highly nervous condition, then you might conceivably believe yourself to be locked in. And if fear could do that to you, couldn't it equally well persuade you that someone was trying to knock you off some steps or make you inhale chlorine gas?

I surveyed the area round the W.C. pan. I sat on the bathroom stool and imagined myself as Caroline in her chair and tried to judge what she would have been capable of. If the bottle of fluid had been on the floor or on the stool she could have reached it from her chair, and even if it had been on the window-sill she could probably have propped herself up for long enough to move it to a position where she could reach it when she sat down again. And she could have put it on the floor and pushed it back of the bowl – perhaps using one of her crutches. Or it might have fallen sideways and rolled there. Janet hadn't said, as far as I could remember, whether the bottle had been standing upright or lying on its side when her hand encountered it.

That would have been on the Sunday I spent with Lesley. It was no use thinking about that and starting up a fresh train of guilt. I must keep to the matter in hand. My parents had gone for a drive after lunch and Caroline hadn't wanted to. There was nothing sinister in that. She had been feeling unwell all that week. So she'd not been up to her usual activity and while my parents were out she had had to use the bathroom. Perhaps she was finding this more difficult than she used to. Perhaps there was some deterioration in her powers of movement that I, at least, knew nothing about.

Perhaps I had believed her to be more capable of doing things than she actually was and perhaps Janet had believed the same. And Caroline, desperately clinging to her few shreds of independence, had tried to encourage this belief and had tried to leave the bathroom as she would wish it to be left; but she had failed and had swallowed her pride and gone to ask Janet because there was nobody else in the flat to ask.

Wasn't this at least as plausible as the devilish plot to make Janet mix the two types of cleaner? Why should Caroline suppose, as the Inspector had said, that Janet would rush off to the kitchen to fetch the powder? And Janet herself had admitted that she always used the other washplace whenever possible, so it was more than likely that she hadn't been in the bathroom at all the previous day and didn't know that we were currently using a liquid cleaner. But Caroline couldn't have known about this quirk of Janet's. Or could she?

There was a rattle at the door. I got up to unbolt it. I'd been in there quite a time and had temporarily forgotten that other people might have more usual reasons for wanting to come in. Mrs Dring gave a slight start when she saw me.

'Are you all right?' she asked. 'That eye of yours looks bad still.'

'I'm fine,' I replied. 'I only wondered if I could find something to put on it to make it less conspicuous.'

I prodded around among the bottles in the cupboard as if this was indeed what I had been doing. Mrs Dring came to my help. I debated for a moment whether to pump her about the lavatory cleaner, but decided that it would only start her wondering and would probably yield little result. There was one thing I could surely mention, however.

'That door's getting awfully difficult to open,' I said. 'The latch is slipping badly. Shall I try and fix it.'

'I shouldn't mess about with it if I was you,' she replied. 'The man's coming in the morning.'

'But it's been like this for ages. Why didn't someone do something about it before?'

'Hush now, Mr Richard. Don't you talk so loud. You'll wake Caroline.'

I lowered my voice. 'But honestly, Mrs D. —'

'Yes, I know. We know things don't always get done here the moment they ought to be done, but things ain't all that easy in this household. All the same we hadn't forgotten and the man was sent for twice and never turned up so if he lets us down again maybe you'd have a go at it —'

'I'd have done it before,' I cried and then caught myself up. Actually I'm not frightfully good with tools. Maybe they preferred to spare themselves my bunglings. 'All the same,' I said lowering my voice, 'it's very unsatisfactory. Someone might easily think they'd got locked in.'

'We was aware of that,' said Mrs Dring sharply. 'We made Caroline promise always to let us know when she was using the bathroom so we could make sure she was all right.'

'I'm not thinking of Caroline,' I muttered and then again I paused. What had I actually said about Janet in my excitement last night? Had my mother taken it in at all? Had she told Mrs Dring? It didn't look like it.

'Anyway,' I went on, 'what's happened to the key? There used to be a key here.'

'Your Mum put it in the kitchen drawer. It wasn't doing no good and we thought it safer because of Caroline.'

My heart seemed to miss a beat: Caroline – and the key.

'Look here, Mrs D.,' I said, controlling myself with an effort, 'what *is* all this about Caroline?'

She looked at me with an unfathomable expression and then said. 'There ain't much to tell really, but you come in the kitchen and I'll tell you.'

We sat at the yellow-topped kitchen table, drinking the strong sweet tea for which I am always ready at any hour, with the door shut so that our voices didn't disturb the others.

'There ain't much to tell, not really,' said Mrs Dring again.

'But you were worried about Caroline using the bathroom,' I said. 'You never used to be so worried about it.'

'Well you see, we always thought her arms and hands were quite all right. Very steady, sort of making up for things a bit. But now – well we ain't quite so sure.'

I must have shown some of the horror I felt. 'What d'you mean? Aren't so sure? What's the matter with her hands?'

'That's just the trouble. We don't rightly know. We only got wondering when your Mum said why didn't she do some knitting for once and Caroline didn't get mad at her but just cried a bit. That's not like her at all.'

'But hasn't someone asked her?'

'That's just the trouble. She won't talk about it. She's trying hard not to let on about it – pretending she's been clumsy or forgetful. Not a word will she say, not to your Dad nor the doctor nor nobody.'

'But this is intolerable!' I cried. 'If there's something the matter with Caroline's arms or hands then she's got to have it seen to at once. She can't lose the use of her arms! She can't! She *can't*!'

Mrs Dring stirred her cup for a moment without replying and then she shook her head and said: 'It ain't all that easy. Maybe it's all right. Maybe it ain't. But she don't want to know. Maybe it's best for her that she don't know.'

'But something's got to be done —'

'Maybe there ain't nothing to be done.'

'Oh God!' I rubbed a hand over my forehead. 'Does Dad know?'

'He knows and yet he don't if you see what I mean. He knows your Mum's worried and he can see for himself. But when he spoke to Caroline and tried to have a look at her she swore stiff there was nothing the matter and snapped his head off. You know how she is.'

'Did Janet know, then?'

'No, I reckon your cousin didn't know nothing about it. Your Mum and I – we're the only ones who see how it is with Caroline and we could be wrong. And with your Mum sick herself – your cousin had to know that and we didn't reckon there was any cause to tell her about Caroline too.'

'And what about me?' I asked very quietly. 'Don't you think it would have been a good idea to say something to me? You could have trusted me never to mention it to Caroline but it would have been useful to me to know. It would have meant I could be more considerate. It would have saved me from being dreadfully mistaken – it would have saved both me and her from what happened yesterday —'

Mrs Dring looked at me in consternation. 'I reckon you ought've been told. I reckon it was a mistake not to let you know.'

'You're flaming right it was a mistake! What I've been thinking – what I've been doing – what I very nearly did!

Christ!' I had to get up and move around the small space
of the kitchen; I didn't know how to bear it, sitting still.
'I wish I were dead,' I said.

'Now don't say that, Mr Richard,' said Mrs Dring
looking up at me, 'don't you go saying things like that – a
fine young chap like you.'

I turned round suddenly to look at her and I could see
her recoil at the expression on my face. I fought with
myself to speak calmly.

'It's all right, Mrs D.,' I said, 'you needn't worry that
I'm going to do anything daft. Last night was enough to
be going on with. Thanks for telling me about Caroline.
I won't breathe a word of course. If anyone wants to
know where I am tell them I've gone shopping.'

There was still an hour or so till closing time. I bought
masses of flowers for Caroline and I combed the book-
shops for new thrillers and the department stores for new
word games and the mathematical games she was so
good at.

At first she received my offerings with feebly uttered
sarcasms and looks of contempt, but I persevered and
eventually regained her confidence enough for her to
agree to try out one of the board games before she
settled down to sleep. She mastered the rules at once of
course, but as usual I was not very good at it and the fact
that I was so closely watching her hands all the time made
me stupider than ever.

Since my conversation with Mrs Dring the see-saw in
my mind had come down with a great thump on the
side of Caroline's innocence and my guilt and self-
loathing had been nagging at me like toothache. The
only way to endure myself was to do everything I
possibly could to make up to Caroline. That she could

lose the strength in her hands was too horrible to contemplate; it would condemn her to a life of total dependence and mean the end of her studies and of any sort of career.

I was going to watch her and judge for myself, and if I believed there was any foundation for my mother's and Mrs Dring's suspicions, then I was going to insist on something being done. I couldn't think what my father was up to, taking no action. A conversation that I had had not so very long ago with my mother came into my head: she had complained that Dad would do nothing. I thought she had been referring to psychiatric treatment, but obviously I had been wrong.

So I found myself watching the way Caroline moved the red and blue counters across the board. It lay on a bed-table, adjusted to the most convenient position for her to reach. I sat alongside, in much the same position as I had the day before, gripping my hands together except when I was actually making a move and staring with great concentration at the board. It was a frightfully complicated game where the letters had number values and you had not only to make words but to ensure that they were so placed as to add up to a correct total. Caroline took only a few seconds to see the best move. But if her brain was quick, her hands moved languidly. She had good, capable hands. The long fingers were very flexible, the nails strong and well-shaped. It seemed hardly credible that there could be anything the matter with them and yet Mother and Mrs Dring were unlikely to have made it up and I remembered her awkwardness when she had handed me the shorthand books. She seemed to be moving with far less than her usual certainty now.

I glanced up at her face. I could see nothing in it

except the usual faint lines of tension, now aggravated perhaps by impatience at my slowness. I did begin to wonder whether she was exaggerating her weakness for my benefit, as a reproach for my attack·on her, but I didn't yet suspect her of anything more. I blundered on. I moved one of my counters to the worst possible position, one that would instantly give her the game. I saw my mistake straight away and was going to ask if I might take it back. But she was too quick for me. Her hand shot out with no weak and uncertain gesture, grabbed my counter and dumped it down on another space, a much cleverer move. Then it instantly withdrew.

I looked up at her again and our eyes met. She flushed a deep red and bit her lip. 'I'm sorry,' she said. 'I didn't mean to play for you. I just couldn't help it.'

'I'm sorry too,' I replied. 'I wish I could give you a better game. Shall we stop now? Aren't you rather tired?'

The dark colour slowly faded from her face. Her hands moved feebly foward and pushed the counters together.

'Yes, we'd better stop,' she muttered. 'I'm rather sleepy. Not too tired to think, but it's rather an effort —'

Her voice trailed away. This was natural enough. I must have hurt her throat quite badly yesterday. But I'd done her no other harm. I was absolutely certain of that. And she had seemed to be wanting to make peace with me. She had even commiserated with me over my black eye and sore knuckles. I wasn't to be made to suffer too much for my own behaviour and yet I was to be made to understand that she was very helpless, more so even than previously.

And then she had slipped up and briskly played my move. She wasn't embarrassed because she'd shown up my own slowness. Not Caroline. If she were on her death bed she would still not care a damn about that. So it could only be that she had realised all along that I was watching her movements and that she felt she had given herself away. She might be deserving of great pity and I might have cruelly misjudged her, but that still didn't alter her character. Caroline never goes crimson with shame or guilt because she has hurt somebody else; Caroline only shows emotion like that when she is furious with herself. The implications were inescapable. She was putting on an act.

I cleared the game away and arranged her pillows, terrified that I too might give myself away, trying to behave as I always had done when she was going through a bad patch and I was sorry for her, but feeling myself to be a hypocrite now as well as a swine.

'Thanks, Dickie,' she said in her weak little voice. 'Would you ask Mother to come in later?'

I promised to do so and added: 'I tell you what. I'll see if anyone at college can come along and give you a better game.'

She refused at once. It was one of Caroline's tragedies that she could not make personal friends. She was on amicable enough terms with other students, but her combination of exceptional intelligence with great physical disability seemed to make close relationships too difficult. However, she agreed to my next suggestion, which was that I should invite Brian again. He's a whizz at intellectual games and I had my own reasons for once more seeking his aid.

That night I could again find no rest. I was right back on the teetering see-saw; the revolving stage had come full circle and there wasn't even the comfort of knowing I had fresh evidence to produce the following day. I had evidence all right, but it wasn't of the sort that anyone else would believe and I would have to test it further before I myself was convinced beyond all doubt.

Caroline was pretending that she was having difficulty in moving her arms and hands. That was my hypothesis. If it was true then it could be for only one reason: to refute what Janet had written in her diary – which she must surely have deciphered – and to cover herself against all suspicion. But she was doing it very cleverly. It looked as if she had even laid the foundation for it before the attacks on Janet began by allowing both my mother and Mrs Dring to suspect her increased weakness while at the same time pretending to be trying to conceal it. And now that she knew I must have read the diary she would have every motive to try to convince me too.

But she didn't know that I had lost the diary. She was more nervous of me than she need be, for in fact the case against her now rested on my word alone and the Inspector had already shown me how very little use that was in the way of proof. But perhaps after all he had not completely disbelieved me. Even though he had turned the set round for me to see the other side they would still have to look into my story, and even if they didn't find Janet's body in the canal they might find some other clue. Although of course even if they did find Janet, that still didn't prove that Caroline was guilty. Probably there never would be any proof, but it would be worth while showing up her pretence about her weakness, all the same.

One question went round and round in my head all night: what did my father really think? To deceive him over a symptom of illness, physical or mental, would surely be beyond the powers even of Caroline, even allowing for the strength of his feeling towards her. Mother had complained that he would take no action.

Did this mean he suspected and was tacitly backing her up? Or could he conceivably have another reason? And above all, if he were to be told the whole contents of Janet's diary, which so far as I knew the Inspector had not yet communicated to him, would this determine him to protect Caroline more than ever, or would his conscience force him, at whatever cost to himself, to come down on my side?

When the dark square of my window showed grey in the early summer dawn I fell asleep at last. I dreamt that I was struggling to find a firm footing at the top of a crumbling cliff and I held out my hands for Janet to cling to, but they were shrivelled and trembling and had no strength in them. I could hear her cry out piteously as she fell. But there was another voice crying my name, an urgent, anxious voice, very real, very near.

'Richard! Are you awake? Please help! Richard!'

I jerked into wakefulness. It was Caroline's voice, faint but distinguishable, from her room next door. I shot out of bed and into the passage. She'd got a bell beside her that rang in my parents' room. Why hadn't she rung it? I pushed open the door. She was lying on the rug by the bed, trying without avail to raise herself. I lifted her back on to the bed.

'Thank God you heard, oh thank God you heard!' she cried as she clung to me.

'Are you all right?' I asked. 'D'you want to get up?'

She shook her head. 'I've just been to the loo. I was getting back into bed. My hand slipped.' She lay back as if exhausted, her arms loosely at her sides. 'Don't tell Mum or Dad,' she added. 'They'd only worry.'

'All right,' I replied and as I spoke I wondered why her words seemed so familiar. Then it came in a flash: Janet's diary. This was exactly what she had said to Janet after running her chair at the stepladder and swearing it was because her hand had slipped. Janet hadn't believed it. I didn't believe it now. But I would have to pretend to.

'Can I get you anything?' I asked.

'What's the time?'

'About half past six.'

'Oh Lord. Ages till breakfast. I don't want to fall asleep again. I'm having frightful nightmares.'

'That's odd,' I said and our eyes met as they had done the evening before, 'very odd. So am I.'

But she had herself well in hand now. Her face was expressionless. 'I suppose you weren't thinking of making tea,' she said.

'All right.' I moved over to the door. 'I won't be very long.'

I didn't even bother to glance back at her. I had learnt all I needed to know. I could even make a guess at what her own bad dreams had been. Maybe it was some sort of telepathy. It's a strange thing about brothers and sisters who are brought up together. They may love each other, be indifferent to each other, perhaps even hate each other. But the fact remains that in some ways they know far more about each other than any other groups of people do. More than parents know of their children or children of their parents; more than close friends, more even than husbands and wives.

I found my mind roaming back over my childhood as I stood by the cooker in the kitchen waiting for the kettle to boil. My earliest memory was of Caroline as a clutching toddler, snatching from me my favourite toy, a well-worn stuffed spotted dog. My parents, always fair, had insisted that she give it back. She had done so, but only after getting hold of some scissors and tearing at the beady eyes and poking out some of the stuffing.

She had been suitably reproved and I had been given other toys.

But it hadn't helped at all. I had been utterly disconsolate. Timmy was sewn up again but it was never the same. Something I had cared for had been damaged and destroyed for ever. And that was why she had done it; not because she wanted the toy but because she wanted to hurt me. She hadn't yet learnt to make effective use of words and she could get at me in no other way.

Sixteen years later and it was just the same. My father might blind himself and my mother be taken in, and Inspector Soames might argue rationally and if it came to a court of law no doubt the scales of justice themselves would swing down on my sister's side. But I knew, as surely as if I had seen it happen in front of my very eyes, that Caroline had tried to kill Janet because I loved her.

And she knew that I knew, and she was very afraid, and was fighting with every weapon at her command.

11

S H E had weapons in plenty. Weakness and pathos and my father's love; and my own guilt and my love for my parents. She'd got me caught in a fine but unbreakable net, tightly woven by the strands of human feeling. My only release would be through visible proof and if the police found nothing then there was only one hope left. I had meant to wait until Brian came before calling Caroline's bluff about her hands; I had been going to ask him to use his persuasion on her to let herself be examined, and I had not meant to mention it to my parents until then. But my mother forestalled me. She must have heard me get up and go to Caroline's room and then to the kitchen. She came in just as I was picking up the tray.

'What happened to Caroline?' she asked in very worried tones. 'She looks dreadful but she won't tell me anything.'

'She's all right,' I replied. 'We both woke early and she called out to me as I came past.'

'I'll take her tea.' My mother touched my arm and I put down the tray. 'In a minute,' she added, and then she poured out a cup for herself and one for me. 'Are you quite sure she was all right?' she asked, seating herself on the kitchen stool and looking up at me unhappily.

'Yes, Mother. Yes, darling. I promise you.'

I nodded and smiled at her. She rubbed her hand across her eyes.

'If she were to be further crippled – if she can't even get herself about – oh God, I don't know how to bear it!'

She looked up at me again. She wasn't crying but there was a blank misery in her face that was even worse.

I had believed myself to have conquered the urge to go for Caroline. I thought I had settled down into a cold, restrained rage that could scheme and wait but would not break out into violence. But I had been wrong. When I saw the look on my mother's face and realised what Caroline was doing to her, and with no higher motive than the covering up of her own crime, the fury came rushing through me again and I didn't know how to keep my voice steady.

I sat on the edge of the kitchen table and put an arm round her shoulders. 'You're to stop worrying, Mother,' I said. 'There's nothing the matter with Caroline. She's putting it on. And I know why.'

I hadn't meant to say it. It was forced out of me. I couldn't bear to see my mother look like that. She did begin to cry then, very quietly, and between sobs she reproached herself for having shown me her anxiety.

'It's bad enough for you as it is,' she said. 'I didn't want you to worry too – to feel you are even more tied to home than ever.'

After a while she calmed down. 'Why do you think Caroline is putting it on?' she asked.

'In order to prove she couldn't have done something rather beastly that I'm quite sure she did do,' I replied.

'Oh Richard! Not – not that sparrow!'

I nodded. I had nearly gone too far. I didn't want to tell Mother about Janet's diary and was glad of this interpretation which would let me out.

'Dad was terribly upset about that,' she said sadly. 'I suppose it could be possible that she is playing us up.'

'She certainly is. And you're not to worry.' I bent to kiss her. 'You take Caroline's tea in now and don't take any notice of what she says or how she looks. Promise me, darling.'

'I'll try.' She wiped her eyes, got up, and poured out Caroline's tea. I moved forward to open the door for her but just before I did so she looked up at me again. 'Richard – now that you know all about it, do you think you could ask your father? He won't listen to me. He thinks I'm fussing. D'you think you could persuade him to have a specialist examine Caroline? I'd be so much happier. Dad might pay some attention to you. He thinks a lot of you, you know.'

I couldn't get out of it. I was caught tight in the net. There was to be no waiting for Brian's help and advice. All I could do was to postpone it for a few hours by saying I wouldn't worry Dad over breakfast but would try and speak to him in the evening.

But at least that gave me a chance to talk to someone else outside the family and the best person was obviously the police Inspector. I could still approach him on the pretext of wanting to know whether they had found my stolen wallet.

'I've been expecting you,' he said when after several unsuccessful attempts to contact him I at last found him in. 'We've no good news for you, I'm afraid.'

I waited. I wasn't sure what he was referring to.

'We think we know who stole your money but there isn't a hope of recovering it.' He paused a moment. 'Nor the little notebook, either.'

I glanced up. He looked tired and rather unhappy, not at all the unhelpful, coldly rational being that he had seemed to me the day before.

'Have you been looking for it?' I asked and must have shown my surprise.

'We have indeed. But it's hopeless. They might have thrown it anywhere when they found it was of no use to them. Since we appear to have little chance of using it as evidence I wonder whether you would care to write out a transcript of it, as far as you can remember? No need to make a sworn statement. It's just for reference.'

'I'd like to very much.' I felt embarrassed. I had been rather taking it for granted that Inspector Soames was pursuing a policy of hushing things up. 'Can I do it here? Or shall I go home and bring it in later?'

'You can do it here if you can find something to write on in our miserably overcrowded accommodation. I have to go out shortly, so let me ask you one or two things first. Will you make a charge?'

'A charge? Oh, you mean my wallet. Do I have to?'

It all seemed frightfully trivial and tiresome. I didn't want to be bothered with coming to court to give evidence. There were far more important things to be getting on with. 'It was only a couple of quid,' I went on. 'It's the diary that really mattered. And after all, it was my fault. I was fighting too.'

'All right then. We'll drop that part. Now to your family troubles. Have you managed to extract any more information out of your sister?'

Once again I looked at him in amazement. 'Did you expect me to?'

He smiled suddenly, a nice crinkly smile that transformed the long melancholy face. 'Yes, my lad, I did expect it. You were right on your mettle when you left here yesterday, weren't you?'

'So all that special pleading for Caroline – that was just to set me off investigating all the more? And not out of consideration for my father or anything like that?'

'Suspected crimes within close-knit families are

notoriously difficult things to handle,' said the Inspector sententiously, 'and professional and intellectual families are the worst of the lot. There was much more chance of you finding out something more at this stage than if I were to come blundering in.'

'But I might have believed your case for Caroline and done nothing! Or I might even have gone for her again!'

He shook his head. 'No. You wouldn't have done nothing. Not feeling as you do about it. And I reckoned you wouldn't do anything silly in the way of actual attack. You've had enough of that to last you for a while.'

'Oh hell, you really are a bloody psychologist, aren't you?' I cried disrespectfully, and then hastily apologised.

He waved it aside, but I thought he looked rather pleased all the same. 'Well. Did you get anywhere?' he asked.

'Only in my own mind. It'd sound damned silly to anyone else.'

'Never mind. Go on.'

So once again I held forth while he listened carefully. 'What on earth can I say to my father?' I concluded. 'I've promised Mother so I'll have to do it. But I don't like it at all. We've got a sort of unspoken truce on at the moment about Caroline, Dad and I. If I once break it then I shall blurt everything out. Janet's diary and all. I know I shall.'

'I shouldn't worry about that,' said the Inspector. 'I told him about the diary myself.'

'Then what the hell's he playing at?' I cried.

'I wouldn't presume to judge. And I don't think you'd better either.'

'I'm damned well going to tackle him, all the same.'

'May I advise you to go very carefully?' said the Inspector. 'Though you might perhaps like to mention one thing when your sister is present. We're dragging the canal tomorrow. I'm very sorry it can't be today, but I couldn't get the men. I'm afraid it's another day of suspense for you but although it may be a matter of life or death it's not exactly a matter of extreme urgency. Unfortunately.'

'Unfortunately,' I repeated bitterly. 'It doesn't take days to drown.' And then I added: 'Can I be there? I won't be a nuisance. And I'd like to know at once if —' I gulped and went on. 'If you do find her.'

'I can't stop you,' he replied, 'but I'd rather you weren't. Take a day away from it. Go in the country. Get some fresh air. You'll feel better afterwards. Or go over to Chelsea and look up your college friends who live in Cheyne Walk.'

I stared at him. 'How d'you know I've got any friends from college who live in Cheyne Walk?'

He smiled again. 'You don't qualify as a detective yet although you've got some of the qualities of a very good one. One has to take every single possibility into account, you know. Even the most remote ones. I'm surprised your friends never told you of our enquiries.'

'I haven't seen them lately,' I muttered. 'Not since my Finals. We had a couple of drinks together then – after the last practical.'

'You did indeed. As several others bear out. The day Miss Packington disappeared. And you left them at approximately twenty past six, which would leave you enough time – though cutting it rather fine – to get back across London and arrive home when you did.'

'So you thought I might have made away with Janet, did you?'

'We thought it not impossible.' He corrected me quietly. 'That sort of thing does happen, you know.'

'Am I clear now, then? Or am I suspected of chucking her into the canal? I could have done it after I got home, you know. Caroline couldn't have stopped me. She's scared stiff of me. Maybe I attacked her in order to shut her up. Maybe I made up this rigmarole about Janet's diary in order to divert attention from myself and on to Caroline. Maybe you're just kidding me along.' I was talking wildly and knew that I was. 'Am I supposed to know that you're going to find Janet's body in the canal? Don't you think you'd better have me there after all? Wouldn't you like to shock me into a confession?'

'Take it easy, take it easy,' said the Inspector. 'All this is very distressing and when you've simmered down a little I'm quite sure you'll be able to see all the flaws in any hypothetical case that you may care to build up against yourself. I'd be grateful for the transcript of that diary. And let me know if you get any useful reactions about the canal. I can only repeat that I am extremely sorry it wasn't done before, and remind you that until you found the notebook there was nothing whatever to indicate that Miss Packington had not left the flat by the usual way.'

He was perfectly right, of course. I realised this when I settled down in a corner of the typists' room to write out the diary. And obviously they had had to investigate me too.

I finished my task, left the police station, and began to wander about aimlessly, avoiding only those streets that would lead me to the waterside. The day seemed to drag ahead interminably and then there was the night to get through as well, and some hours of the next day too. I pictured them finding her body. I calculated the number of hours it must have been in the water and assessed the condition in which it would probably be found, with a sort of obsessional accuracy, almost as if I were answering an examination question.

And then suddenly there came a sickening revulsion and I quickened my steps in a futile attempt to escape my thoughts. If I went on like this I would drive myself crazy. The Inspector was right; I'd better keep out of the way tomorrow. But not on a delightful country ramble. I was passing the entrance to our local Labour Exchange. I went in, found they were seeking temporary labourers for demolition work, and signed on to start on a near-by site that very afternoon. In the days when obtaining my degree had seemed the main shadow on the horizon, it had been my intention to have a short holiday immediately after Finals and then take any old job for a few weeks while looking for something permanent in the industrial research line. But since Janet had gone, all motive and sense of purpose had gone too and no one at home had reproached me for my drifting. It was time I replenished my dwindling savings, though, and the more strenuous the work, the better. And this was something where one could put in as many or as few hours as one wanted to.

I felt a little better after leaving the Labour Exchange, but not up to going back home yet. In particular, I didn't want to be with Caroline and be obliged to assume that compassion and affection which for a few hours the previous day I had genuinely felt. There is something particularly repulsive about having a sincere burst of remorse exploited like this; almost as if you were having your deepest feelings kicked right back in your face. So I telephoned instead and told my mother what I was doing and promised to be in for the evening. And then I went and bashed away amid stinking clouds of dust with a miscellaneous assortment of navvies of all ages and sizes and colours and creeds. There were even a few other students.

I was surprised and rather chagrined to find how soon I got tired, but it wasn't the sort of situation where one shows such signs of human weakness so I just went on getting stiffer and stiffer until most of them knocked off for the day. When I got home I lay in the bath for twenty minutes or more in a state of unthinking bliss. And my afternoon's activities provided a very useful safe topic of conversation over the dinner-table. My mother hoped I wasn't doing anything dangerous but my father was rather amused when I said I felt as if I was going to collapse after the first hour and a half of it.

'Unaccustomed use of muscles,' he said. 'It'll wear off tomorrow.'

'Gosh, I hope so.'

'Anyway, it gets rid of his aggressions,' said Caroline. 'It's better than having him work them off on me.' She gave me a spiteful glance as she spoke. It was just as it had always been except that I knew now what she had done.

And I was watching the way she moved. We were eating a sort of rice concoction that didn't require cutting up but that was simply shovelled in with a fork. Caroline was doing that all right. But no particular effort was required, and I wished it had been steak. On the other hand there had been even less effort required to push the counters across the board and yet Caroline had gone crimson with confusion when I had seen her pounce so briskly and neatly on one of them. She was going to have one hell of a job of it if she really was going to keep up this pretence. I wondered whether she'd been keeping it up all day. I hadn't had a chance yet to ask my mother.

After dinner we went along to the waiting-room to have coffee, as we often do, and I noticed that my father pushed Caroline's chair. There wasn't anything significant in this, however, since one of us usually did push her chair when we were going in the same direction. I stayed to help Mother clear up and make the coffee, and when we came to the front of the flat we found that Caroline was out of her chair and lying propped up on the sofa and my father was sitting near her, talking earnestly. Mother had reminded me of my promise and I wished I hadn't given it. I was becoming more and more apprehensive every minute about speaking to my father.

In the event it all turned out quite differently from expected. We were drinking coffee and talking in a desultory way about our neighbours and Caroline had just picked up her second cup of coffee and was holding it cradled in her lap.

'I'm afraid we're going to have cranes and bulldozers and a terrible noise going on at the back later this year,' said my mother. 'Mrs Anderson says they're going to start building there in September.'

We made various complaining noises but nobody said anything in particular.

'Still, it will be a good thing when it's all cleared up,' my mother went on. 'Particularly if they do tidy up the canal and make a nice waterside walk as they have in some other places.'

I thought I saw Caroline shift slightly on the sofa. And suddenly the Inspector's remarks made that morning came back to me. In my preoccupation with the problem of speaking to my father I had temporarily forgotten them.

'They're dragging the canal tomorrow,' I said. 'Inspector Soames told me. They think Janet might have fallen in there.'

I suppose my parents knew about this already but they had obviously been keeping it from Caroline. I don't know which came first, the loud cry she uttered or the falling coffee-cup. She must have been putting it back on the little table beside her because that was where it fell, spreading its dark brown stains on the pale cream of the sofa and the beige background of the Indian carpet.

My parents rushed to her side. She was crying convulsively.

'I can't bear it! I can't, I can't! Oh God help me – they're going – my hands – they're going too! I can't move. I can't move at all! Oh God help me, God help me!'

It was terrible to hear. I stood by helplessly while my parents knelt down and tried to soothe her. I didn't doubt her guilt. And yet I felt shaken and weak with pity and horror. If this was acting, then it was of a standard that one seldom has the privilege to see. At last my parents stood up and my father motioned to Mother and me to leave the room.

We went back to the kitchen. 'Cold water. That's for coffee stains, isn't it?' said my mother in a dazed way.

I pushed her gently down on to the stool. 'Never mind the carpet now,' I said, 'there are worse things than ruined carpets.'

'I know.' She got up again and began to rummage in the cupboard where the cleaning things are kept. 'I know. And I don't want to think about them.'

I had to let her comfort herself in her own way, which was to take out bottles and then immediately put them back again. I didn't feel capable of doing anything better myself. I'd exploded a mine and there was no knowing what the outcome would be.

So we hung about the kitchen, Mother and I, not speaking to each other again until at last my father came into the room.

'Oh – that's where you are,' he said. 'She's quiet now. I've given her a strong sedative. We'll leave her a little and get her to bed later. I'm sorry about the carpet, Phyl. I know you're particularly fond of it.'

How they will harp on unimportant things, I thought angrily; can't they face the facts for once, however intolerable.

But my strictures were unjust. My mother snapped right out of her futile activity, clasped her hands together as if to steady them, and looked straight at Dad. One forgets how beautifully she stands, how lovely she can look when for once in a while she sheds the role of harassed housewife.

'Please, Andrew,' she said, 'please don't keep me in suspense any longer. Nor Richard either. It's not fair on us. Please answer my question honestly. Is there anything wrong with Caroline? Physically, I mean. Is there any reason to suppose she is going to be even more disabled than she is at present?'

'I don't know what to think. I only wish I could answer you.' My father was frowning heavily and looked genuinely puzzled.

'But you must *know*! For pity's sake, Andrew, let us know too.'

'I don't know,' he replied, and then added testily: 'Medicine doesn't know everything. Practically nothing, in some cases. In this case, for instance. Call in a dozen specialists and they'll all give different opinions. It's probably psychosomatic. That's about all they'll be agreed on. Which means precisely nothing, except that body and mind are inextricably linked together. As far as I can see she has many of the symptoms of a myatonic complaint – one of the degenerative muscle diseases. They're not very common. Which is just as well since there's not much you can do about them. I wouldn't have thought it would follow on polio but I'm not an expert and I suppose it could happen. On the other hand she is in many ways a typical hysteric. And when it comes to physical symptoms produced by hysteria it's a case of you name it, we'll find it. Hysterical blindness, hysterical deafness, hysterical digestive upsets, hysterical paralysis —'

'But she is paralysed,' I broke in.

'Oh yes. That's certain enough. No hope of any improvement there.'

'I can't believe you've no opinion at all,' said my mother. 'Even if you're not sure, you must incline to one view or the other. If it were a patient of yours, for instance. You'd have to say something then.'

'Good God, woman, what d'you want me to say!' cried my father furiously. 'I'm not a magician. D'you want me to pull out a pack of lies? D'you want me to play the know-all? You wanted an honest answer. I've told you. I don't know.'

'Then we'll have to take her to a specialist,' said my mother. 'One who'll be able to tell whether she really has got this mya- thing, this muscle disease.'

'We could do that,' he agreed, 'but only if she wants to. At the moment she doesn't. She dreads it. And I don't blame her.'

'But Andrew, she'll *have* to go. You'll have to insist.'

'Insist on her being made the subject of painful experimentation? Put her into the power of a lot of vultures gobbling away at an interesting case to write a learned article on? No, thank you. I'm not doing that.'

'But you took me to various specialists. And it was worth it. I'm getting better.'

'You are, thank God. That was different. There was no doubt about the diagnosis. Only as to the treatment.'

My mother was silenced and I could think of nothing to say either. I could see my father's point in a way, but he was being singularly unhelpful. And I couldn't help but suspect him of another motive.

'I think, dear, we'll just have to watch and wait for the time being,' he went on more gently, obviously repenting of his ill-temper. 'Things have been very difficult all round lately and she may well improve when the situation is clarified. Meanwhile all we can do is to try and spare her any additional strain or shock. All of us.'

He glanced at me as he spoke and I knew he was blaming me for mentioning the dragging of the canal. I'd never have done it if the Inspector hadn't suggested it and it seemed to me to be monstrously unfair. I was strung up to an intolerable pitch; the slightest touch would set me off.

'You needn't worry,' I cried. 'I'm not going to attack Caroline again. Though God knows I've cause to, considering what she's done to me.'

'Richard,' said my mother warningly, but I paid no attention to her and went storming on, glaring at my father:

'Whose fault is it there's strain and shock? Who brought it all upon us? Caroline, of course. She's tortured Janet to death. She's killed the only girl I'll ever care for. And you'll do nothing about it – you'll only take her side. It doesn't matter how I feel – it doesn't matter how she's tormented me. It's only Caroline who matters. It always has been. She's ruined my life, she could kill me too and you wouldn't care. She's killed my girl and all you do is sit on the fence till someone accuses her and then you'll take refuge in medicine and swear anything to protect her. Even if it's a lie. You'll lie to protect her – lie – lie – lie!'

I was choking and could say no more. My father swung round to face me.

'Be quiet, you stupid child!' he shouted. 'You know nothing about it!'

I could feel the blood rush to my cheeks and my hands clench into fists at my sides. My mother stepped between us.

'Oh no,' she said quietly but with great firmness. 'Oh no. That's all we are lacking. For you two to quarrel. You shouldn't have said that, Andrew. It's neither true nor fair. He's suffering a lot. He understands only too well.'

She looked at my father reproachfully and he muttered something that could be taken for an apology.

'And now it's your turn, Richard,' my mother went on. 'I will not have you speaking to your father like that, however unhappy you are. Will you please apologise.'

I did so, grudgingly.

'Thank you,' she said, 'and it wouldn't be a bad idea if you would both of you try to show a little more consideration for me. And now I suppose I had better go and put Caroline to bed.'

'And I must do some work,' muttered my father, glancing at his watch and leaving the kitchen immediately after her.

I waited a minute to let them get out of the way and then I went to my room and pulled down a suitcase from the top of the wardrobe and packed it as if I were going for several weeks' holiday. Then I sat down on the end of my bed to think. I could hear Mother moving about in Caroline's room next door. Dad would be writing at his desk. It might be possible for me to make a dash for it and get out of the flat without seeing either of them but it was rather a childish way to do it. And I'd have to go to a hotel for the night because it was too late to find digs. It would be better perhaps to stick it out till the morning and tell my mother, at any rate, that I was going.

12

I FELL asleep instantly and had no dreams. But I awoke feeling unrefreshed, heavy, depressed and apprehensive as I could never remember having felt before. I got up and went along to the kitchen to help Mother make breakfast. Caroline was still asleep, she said; we wouldn't wake her. She wanted to know if I was going back to the demolition-site today and seemed relieved when I said that I was.

'But don't they give you overalls or something, darling?' she added. 'You'll ruin all your clothes.'

At other times I would have told her not to fuss, but at this moment her remark only made me dread more than ever having to tell her I was leaving home.

Dad opened his mail as usual over breakfast and barely acknowledged my presence. But just before he left the room he turned to me and said:

'Don't do your navvying for too long, Richard. I'd like to see you starting off soon in a decent job.'

'I've got an interview with Southern Chemicals next week,' I said.

'Good, good. I hope it goes well. You might even switch over to the personnel side later on. You'd be good at that.'

Then he immediately went on to tell Mother of his day's programme and where he could be reached if there were urgent calls, so I had no chance to reply. In fact I'd have found it difficult to do so, for every moment I was becoming more depressed and more and more inclined to sneak away without saying anything. I couldn't face another scene and I didn't think Mother could either. But somehow or other I had to get my suitcase out of the flat.

In the end I waited until she had shut the front door behind my father and then came straight out with it. I dumped my case on the floor in the hall and pulled her into the waiting-room.

'If they find Janet's body,' I said, 'it means it was Caroline who drove her to drown herself. I can't explain in detail now, but it's true. Inspector Soames believes it. And so does Dad. I'm sure he does. It's absolute hell for Dad, I know, and I'm sorry I got so worked up last night. But it'll be easier for him if I'm out of the way, and for you too, Mother. You won't be torn in two. I won't go far, and probably not for long. It depends what happens. And I'll phone you this evening without fail. Please don't worry, Mother. It's for the best. You know it is.'

She listened to me in silence. 'I don't know how to bear it,' she whispered when I had done, 'that you should be turned out of your own home on top of everything else.'

'It won't be for long. Only till this business is over. Though I think I'll start looking for a permanent place of my own. We can't go on as we did last night. You must see that we can't.'

She wiped her eyes. 'No, I suppose not. I suppose you're right. You always did have good judgement when once you stopped to think. It's one of the many things that Dad has always valued in you.'

I couldn't answer this; it hurt too much.

'He would never tell a lie, darling, you know that,' she went on. 'If Caroline has done anything – not right, then he'll face it. Just as I shall have to do. Your father would never lie.'

'No,' I agreed, 'he wouldn't actually lie. But opinions

can differ – medical ones particularly. He said so himself.
I'm sure he's honestly puzzled about Caroline. But if he
has to state an opinion one can guess what it will be. And
if other doctors are going to be asked too then they're not
going to go against him. Not in his position. Not with his
reputation. They'll stick together like limpets. From
self-interest if not from sympathy. They might need him
to give evidence for them one day.' My voice was rising;
I tried to lower it. 'It'll all be hushed up,' I went on. 'You
can't hit at a man like Dad. Not through a crippled
daughter. They'll say Janet killed herself. Shock and
bereavement – all the bloody lot. All very sad. But soon
forgotten. A poor little orphan. And no one will care. No
one will care a damn what has happened to her except
me – me – me!'

'Hush, darling.' My mother put her arms round me.
'*I* care. I care very much indeed.'

'I know. I'm sorry. I'd better go now. I don't want to
get all worked up again.'

But she held me back. 'Richard – try to hope a
little. Nothing is certain yet. They may not find Janet's
body. Even if she did fall in the water she may have
swum a little and got out. She's not a bad swimmer.
I remember once we talked of it. Try not to give up
hope.'

'Well, where is she then? Why haven't the police found
her?'

'She may have lost her memory. That sometimes
happens. Or she may not want to be found. It's very
difficult to trace someone who's determined to stay
hidden. The police can't go searching every house in the
country.'

'But how would she live? She'd no money. She's not
been seen at any post office or bank.'

'Perhaps she found work. Perhaps someone took pity on her.'

'Oh God, Mother, that would be almost the worst of the lot! Can't you just imagine what sort of 'work', what sort of 'pity' a helpless girl with Janet's looks would find?'

'Don't give up hope,' she repeated quietly. 'There are still decent people left in the world.'

I kissed her and then picked up my suitcase. 'I'll phone this evening. Please explain it all to Dad. And tell Caroline —' I paused a moment. 'Tell Caroline whatever makes it easiest for you.' I paused again. 'I'm sorry. I – I can't leave her my love. Goodbye, Mother.'

I made my escape. It looked as if she was about to cry again and I wasn't far off it myself.

I went first to the demolition site, told the foreman I'd got to look for a room and would be back later. And then I walked slowly along, past streets of shabby lodging houses in decaying terraces. I didn't really care where I went; anything would do as long as it was cheap. I told myself that I would starve rather than ask my father for any money. And yet I didn't ring at any of the doors. It seemed that I had some sort of purpose, although I hardly knew what it was myself.

And then I realised. I was treading the very pavements that I had often walked before when I was going to take refuge with Lesley. She was on a long trip abroad with her parents, I knew that. I wondered who had the flat now and whether there was any hope that, being near vacation, it might be unlet. I rather hoped it was. It would be some little glimmer of comfort to be in familiar surroundings and remember that I'd once been happy there, rather than to be in some drab hotel room.

For once I was in luck. Apparently Lesley's flat-mate had moved out the day before and the landlady, who inhabited the ground floor, had been just about to put it up for re-letting. She recognised me and was willing to let me have it. As Lesley always used to say, she was much more interested in money than in morals but she did like people to look clean and respectable. So that was fine. I can't say that it actually made me feel cheerful, but it did give me the feeling that it was sometimes possible for things to go right. I scattered my few belongings around, went out and bought some essential foods, and decided that I would spend the evening writing a long letter to Brian explaining everything and asking if he'd come and stay with me here instead of at home. That helped a bit too, to have a definite programme for the rest of the day.

When I got to the site I was asked if I'd like to earn danger money and that pleased me too. So I swayed about on crumbling masonry and felt very relieved when the siren sounded. During the breaks I talked to one of the students, a real anarchist type, the sort I usually avoid like the plague, being the conventional and conformist creature that I am. But just at the moment I felt something of an outcast myself and things looked rather different from this angle. He looked terrible, of course, but he was big and well-built and his voice was very snooty and public school. His name was Gabriel, of all things, which he thought was a huge joke and it amused me too. He was reading literature but he didn't think he'd bother to go back to college next term.

'Why are you doing this?' I asked.

'Oh – money. Domestic problems,' he replied airily. 'You too?'

I nodded.

'My father is chairman of a merchant banking house.

We have a little difference of opinion occasionally,' he said.

I laughed again. 'It even happens to me, believe it or not.'

He studied me closely. 'Curious. Very curious,' he said, but didn't ask any more questions.

I liked him. It was pretty obvious that he was experimenting with drugs and he dropped a few hints, but he talked like a normal human being and didn't bother to put on all the jargon and the trimmings. He seemed to like me too.

'See you tomorrow?' he asked when we knocked off.

I nodded.

'Good. It'll enliven the tea-break.'

It was quite an effort when I left the site to remember that I wasn't going home. Thanks largely to Gabriel, the day hadn't been quite as bad as it might have been. There had even been one or two minutes when I hadn't been thinking about Janet.

I went back to Lesley's flat, had a good wash and changed my clothes. I didn't hurry. I was putting off the moment when I would go to the police station. One always says one wants to know the worst, but in fact the feeblest little flicker of hope is better than all hope killed. I could have telephoned, I suppose, but for the same reason I decided to go in person. Now what am I going to do if they have found Janet's body, I kept saying to myself as I walked along; I must have some sort of plan other than writing to Brian; I can't possibly go home – less so than ever; I'll have to get drunk; I wish I'd asked Gabriel where he lived – if in fact he lives anywhere other than on the streets; I'd pinch some of his filthy dope.

I hadn't decided on anything by the time I got to the station. The Inspector was out but the sergeant had a message for me. They hadn't found Janet, but they had found something. They'd dragged up an object that looked like her handbag; it had been wedged between some large stones that had fallen into the water from the crumbling path just beneath our bathroom window.

Where Caroline must have thrown it, I added to myself.

The sergeant couldn't tell me any more, but if I'd like to wait then Inspector Soames might be back. I shook my head. I found it impossible to sit still and I had an over-whelming urge to speak to my mother. I would phone later, I said. I made for the nearest call-box and rang home, praying that my father would be out or would not answer the phone. His voice came on the line at the same time as my mother's did and before I had spoken. They must have picked up the different extension receivers.

'It's all right, Andrew,' I heard my mother say. 'This call will be for me.'

I heard the click as my father put the receiver down and then my mother's voice, urgent and anxious:

'Richard – is that you?'

'I've heard the news,' I said. 'Just the outline. Is it really Janet's bag? What do they think? What are they going to do?'

She began to talk quickly, in a very low voice. I guessed she was in the hall and that she was constantly looking over her shoulder for fear that Dad or Caroline would appear. Yes, it was definitely Janet's bag; but how it had got there and what Janet had done it was impossible to tell. They'd been making a lot more enquiries. Of neighbours, of people at the warehouses backing on to the canal farther along, of the railway authorities, of a group of kids who'd installed themselves in a shed just beyond the broken bit of hoarding opposite the back of our flats.

They were rounding up all the shifting population; they were combing the whole area, going at it all out now, radio and television appeals. The lot.

In fact the full-scale search that I'd so longed for on that day that now seemed an age ago – the day when Janet didn't come home. But it was nobody's fault, I told myself. There'd been no clue. There'd been only the diary, and Caroline had hidden that.

'They'll find her, darling.' My mother's voice was scarcely above a whisper now. 'They're going to find her. It can't be long now. Keep your heart up, my darling. Where can I contact you if I have any news?'

I gave her my landlady's phone number; she was quite good-natured and would take a message in emergency. And then I wanted to ask how Dad was, but I didn't know how to. Mother must have guessed it.

'Your father is all right,' she said. 'He knows and understands it all. And so do I. We have talked it all over with the Inspector. Your father will do what is right, whatever the outcome.' Her voice shook. 'Be kind to him, Richard.'

'And – Caroline?' I had to ask it. I knew Mother would wish me to.

'It's very strange,' came her reply. 'She has been absolutely calm. Not a hint of hysterics. She doesn't mention the search for Janet. I told her you'd had a bit of a disagreement with Dad and she accepted it without a murmur. And there's no sign of weakness in her either.'

This was very odd indeed. I thought about it a lot after saying goodbye to my mother and could make no sense of it. Either Caroline had a perfectly clear conscience after all or she had faced the worst and made her own plans. Perhaps she had simply decided to bluff it out. It would be virtually impossible to prove that she'd had murder in mind. If Janet were after all to be found dead, then Caroline would simply stick to the defence that the Inspector had so clearly mapped out for her; Janet's own phobia had led to her death. And if Janet were found alive, what after all could she tell other than what was in her diary? She might elaborate the details, that was all. It was hardly possible that she could produce any firm evidence of Caroline's guilt. If Caroline's nerve held out then she could carry it through on her own; she wouldn't even need my father's protection. She'd had a very bad moment when I'd said they were dragging the canal, but it looked as if she'd regained her nerve now.

I walked slowly back towards my basement flat. There didn't seem much point in going to the police station again. My heart was full of hope. It would keep bounding in. There had been no need for Mother to urge me to keep up my spirits. Janet's sweet face was constantly before my eyes. If I get her back, I thought, I'll even forgive Caroline; I'll even be sorry for her again. And it couldn't be much longer now.

But there was no more news that night. Nor the next morning, which was Saturday. We finished work on the site at noon. I used the phone in the foreman's hut to ring my mother, learnt that there was nothing fresh, and came back to the entrance to find that Gabriel had not yet gone. Suddenly I felt a great longing for his company. He knew nothing about my personal affairs and cared less. We'd had some fascinating conversations about life and morals and it would pass the time of waiting if we were to continue them. He'd be comforting to be with.

'I've got to go home now,' he said. 'Like to come?'

'Home?' I echoed stupidly, with my thoughts wandering around stately country mansions and luxury seafront penthouses, for I guessed that his people must be very rich.

'"Be it ne'er so humble",' he sang in a quavering falsetto, '"there's no place like" – my nasty little back room which is about ten minutes away from here. I don't usually stay so long in one place but it so happens that I've got a responsibility at the moment.'

We weren't on the sort of terms where one expects to answer very personal questions, so I didn't ask him what it was, though I was mildly curious as we walked along. I'd got a very strong suspicion that something in him wasn't really enjoying this trampish sort of life and that he wouldn't mind going back to his real home. For all his elaborately dirty clothes and his greasy locks there was something fastidious about him. I bet he still keeps pretty clean underneath it all, I said to myself, and I wondered whether he really was hooked on hard drugs. I didn't think it could have been going on very long. I hoped not. I liked him too much.

We came to one of the most dilapidated of the mid-Victorian terraces. It couldn't have been very far away from Lesley's flat, which was now my own, but I'd never actually explored this area. He let me in to a hallway with peeling brown paint on the walls and torn lino on the floor, and pushed open a door that was standing slightly ajar.

'Basement,' he said, leading the way.

I was about to pull to the door behind us when he stretched out a hand to stop me:

'I'm afraid we have to leave it open. Janie doesn't like shut doors.'

'Janie?' I repeated.

'Yes. My responsibility.'

I followed him down the stairs, wondering. A cat? A

dog? Something was stirring within me, making me both agitated and afraid.

He pushed at another door at the bottom of the stairs; it too had been adjusted to remain slightly ajar. We came into a stuffy, sordid little room with the minimum of broken-down furniture.

'Oh,' he said, 'she's not here. She'll have gone to the loo. It's in the back yard. We have sole use of it, fortunately. She'll be quite a time then. It's a very elaborate ritual, going to the loo. First of all we have to prop open all these doors and keep coming back to see that we've done it securely, and then we have to make sure that there is nobody about, and then we have to prop open the loo door and that takes longest of the lot because we have to check again and again that it's quite safe before we can go and perform our natural function. Makes life very complicated, all this open door business. Especially when you've got the opposite to the shut-in thing as well and are afraid to go out. I really don't think I'm going to be able to feed her and look after her any longer. I really do think I'm going to have to do something about Janie.'

The dreary little room was swimming before my eyes. I grabbed his arm. 'Gabriel!' I cried.

He yelled loudly and leapt into the air. 'Leggo, you nincompoop! that's my sore arm! You've got a grip like a tin-opener!'

I let him go. 'Gabriel – quick – this is vital. Where did you find Janie?'

He grumbled at me, rubbing his arm. 'She rose from the water,' he said, 'like Botticelli's Venus. The somewhat noisome waters of one of our unrehabilitated canals. A week or so ago. I happened to be in a rather Hamlet-like condition at the time and had just climbed through a broken hoarding with some sort of notion of ending it all. I'm no swimmer. She was trying to climb out so I gave her a hand. She was positively gibbering. Said someone had just tried to kill her. I couldn't quite see how because there wasn't a sign of another human being on the horizon, so I assumed she'd had the same idea as I had and had since regretted it. So I brought her here. I don't know who the hell she is and there isn't a clue on her and she can't seem to remember herself. She's definitely a case for the headshrinkers and it's not helping her any, lurking down here, especially as I have to keep leaving her in order to go and earn some filthy lucre. She goes into the tizzy of all time when I murmur police or hospital. There might be shut doors, you see. But I've got to do something.'

'Gabriel!' It was all I could do to stop myself grabbing his arm again. 'I know her. She's my cousin – she's my girl! There's a full-scale police hunt on. Don't you read the papers? Don't you see the television?'

'Papers? Television? My dear Dick, what would *I* want with such trivia of the establishment?'

'Oh God, it's too much! Oh God, it's a miracle! She's alive – she's alive!' I could feel the tears burning at my eyes. I could have hugged him. 'Where's the loo?' I cried. 'I'll go and fetch her.'

This time it was he who grabbed hold of me and he spoke in a very sober and serious voice. 'No. Let me break it gently. You'll go smothering her and kill her with the shock. I'll see if she remembers. What's your full name?'

I told him.

'And hers?'

I told him that too. My heart was racing. The yearning to see her seemed to be pulling me to pieces but I knew that he was right. He pushed me back to the door at the bottom of the stairs.

'Wait in the hall and I'll call you. This solves my problem anyway. If all's well you can take her home.'

I took a few steps and then turned back to him. 'My father's a doctor. He'll know what to do.'

'Good. Hurry up now. She's coming back. I hear the waters rushing.'

I stood in the hallway scuffing at the torn lino. One or two other inmates of the house came in and glanced at me without interest. Prostitutes and petty thieves, I thought; minding their own business; probably don't even know there's a girl in the basement who never goes out. At last Gabriel reappeared.

'I've established your bona fides,' he said. 'I wasn't going to hand her over to anybody. She seems to be sorting it out gradually but it's somewhat touch-and-go-ish. Did you say you'd got a doctor in the house?'

'Yes, yes,' I cried impatiently. 'My father. He's a psychiatrist.'

'Then you'd better take her home and hand her over to him right quick. And I wouldn't talk much to her about the past just yet.'

I promised not to. 'But she does remember me?' I asked as we moved down the stairs.

'She does indeed. I gather you are some sort of god incarnate.'

'Gabriel!' I cried. 'Gabriel – you are manna from heaven! You are – I don't know what you are. An angel I suppose.'

'An archangel.' He corrected me gravely. 'No excitements now. She's quite calm at the moment. She's making tea. She says you'd like some.'

There was no need to urge me to caution. From now

on I was going to treat her like porcelain. We pushed open the second door and Gabriel tactfully disappeared into the yard beyond. She came towards me from the corner by the window where the gas cooker stood. She had on the blue and white frock that I had often seen her in. It was crumpled, but quite clean. Her hair was clean too, though not very tidy. There was no mirror and very little facility for carrying out one's toilet in the room. Her face was thin and very pale but the grey eyes were as lovely as ever and the lips were slightly parted.

'Hullo, Jan,' I said and stood still while she brought me the tea in a chipped white cup.

'We've only digestive biscuits,' she said. 'I'm sorry we haven't any cake.'

I felt a funny little twinge within me at the way in which she said that 'we'. I smothered it hastily. One doesn't carp at good Samaritans. One accepts them gratefully. But I did pray that he hadn't put her on to drugs.

'Thanks,' I said. 'How do you do your housekeeping?'

'Here's the tins and things,' she said, opening a dilapidated cupboard, 'and there's the bread bin. The milk goes off in this weather so I'm afraid it's only dried.'

'And where do you wash your clothes?'

'Here at the sink. And they dry in the yard. It gets quite a lot of sun. More than you'd think. I sit there. It's not overlooked. No one can see me. And I've got books to read. But I get muddled sometimes.'

I couldn't speak for a moment, and then I said: 'Do you want to come home with me, Jan?'

She nodded. Her mouth quivered but she didn't speak.

'Well, we'll go just as soon as you feel like it. We'll get a taxi.'

'How far is it?' she asked. 'Could I – could I walk?'

'Not very far. Do you feel strong enough?'

'I'd like to try.'

'All right then. We'll pick up a cab if you get tired.'

'I'd like to see the people in the streets. I've missed them. I don't feel safe, going out alone. And I don't feel right either with—'. She broke off. I noticed how she avoided mentioning Gabriel's name. 'But I think I'll feel safe with you,' she added.

'Good. That's fine.'

Up till now she had been speaking quite calmly, though obviously under considerable stress. Suddenly her control snapped. She caught at one of my hands with both of hers and her eyes searched my face. They were wide and terrified, like a hunted animal.

'Richard – don't leave me! Don't leave me!'

'I'll never leave you,' I said.

She clung to me, trembling. I stroked her hair and began to revise my plans. I had intended to ask Gabriel – who was still nobly sitting it out in the loo – to look after her for a little longer while I phoned home and explained to my father about Janet so that he'd be ready to attend to her the moment we got back. But the way she was holding on to me now made me feel reluctant to leave her for a moment. I might still manage to phone on the way home, but I was afraid that if she came inside the tiny call-box it would upset her precarious balance completely and that she'd be almost as frightened if I left her alone outside it. She really was in a bad way. I could see just what Gabriel had meant.

I continued to stroke her hair and tried to decide what was best. Perhaps Gabriel would do the telephoning for me. After all, I had relieved him of his responsibility and it wasn't much to ask. I hoped I was treating her in the best way possible in the circumstances but I'm afraid I did make a mistake then.

'We'll wait a little longer till he comes back,' I said, cocking my head in the direction of the yard, 'and I'll get him to ring home and tell them we're on the way.'

She trembled more than ever. 'No. Please, no.'

'Why not, Janet?'

She began to talk in a scarcely audible voice, starting sentences and never finishing them. After a moment or two I got the message. The poor kid was dreadfully embarrassed and ashamed. She didn't want my parents to know about Gabriel. She wanted me to make up a convincing story for her so that no one need ever know she had been living with – presumably in every sense of the term – a sort of guardian angel in the shape of a conscientious hippy.

So that was out, too. I still thought I might somehow manage to slip Gabriel my home phone number without Janet seeing, and if he were quick enough on the uptake he would understand what I wanted. But when at last he came in from the yard she clung to me more than ever, and he was so obviously longing to be rid of us that I decided to drop the attempt. He'd certainly deserved his release. He must have had a hell of a worry with her, not to mention being tied to this room and having to do some regular work. No doubt there had been a certain amount of compensation but probably not enough, in his opinion, to make up for the burden. I must admit I'd have hesitated myself to take on Janet in the state she was in, with no help or advice from anyone, and in such frightful living conditions.

So we said good-bye to Gabriel. He told me he wouldn't be going back to the demolition work, but he'd be at this address for another week and would I please let him know how she was. This I promised to do. Then he tilted Janet's face up towards him to kiss her good-bye. Her pale cheeks went pink, and one part of myself seemed to detach itself from the rest and look on with faint amusement, while the other part felt that twinge again. He let her go, shrugged his shoulders, and didn't even bother to come upstairs with us.

We came out into the brightness of the late Saturday afternoon and Janet held on to my arm and looked about her and blinked and then opened her eyes very wide. She was like a newly hatched chick wondering at the world. We moved slowly along.

'You'll tell them something?' She said this several times.

'Yes, love. I'll tell them something.' My mind was already at work concocting some sort of tale if I had to give any explanation in front of Janet. A female Gabriel perhaps; a prostitute with a heart of gold. But of course I would tell them the truth later.

'I'm sorry,' she muttered a little later. 'I couldn't help it.'

I took it she was referring to the same subject. Her memory was still very shaky; she was very obsessed by the last few days. Perhaps it was just as well.

'Of course you couldn't,' I replied. 'It doesn't matter in the least.'

And in spite of the twinge, in some odd way this was true. It didn't matter. Not now. I'd always thought, though God knows why I should imagine I'd got the right to ask it, that I could only want to marry a virgin. But I truly think that if I'd been forced to share Janet with another man, and could choose which one, then it would have been Gabriel whom I would have chosen.

We were silent for a few minutes, while I planned

what to do when we got back. I would ring the bell of the flat and one of my parents would come to the door. I could quickly explain the essentials and make sure that Caroline was kept right out of the way. And then my father would take over and arrange for Janet to go straight to hospital or whatever he thought best.

'Will Uncle be angry with me?' she asked suddenly.

'No, love, no. He'll help you. He'll help you and care for you.'

But once again I seemed to have said the wrong thing. She began to tremble again. It was devilishly difficult. I'd no idea how much she remembered. Perhaps she was worried about seeing my father because she'd remembered how much he cared for Caroline. She hadn't mentioned Caroline yet. I hoped that she would only recall the earlier beastliness; that those last hours in the flat were gone for ever. But her next words dashed this hope.

'I can hear the key turning,' she said in a dazed, low monotone, 'there's always a key turning – a key turning – a key turning.'

She repeated it again and again. I looked down at her face and saw that a dull, vacant look had come into her eyes.

'Yes, love, yes,' I murmured. 'It's all over now. Never anything to frighten you again. Never ever again. You'll talk to my Dad. You'll tell him all about it. You'll feel quite safe then. You'll see.'

I spoke with great confidence but my mind was uneasy. I didn't like the way she looked; I didn't like the way she talked. I'd seen too much of it; in the wards at the hospital, in the faces of patients who came to the consulting-room at home. For the first time I felt a little stab of fear that not all my father's skill and experience would be able to restore full reason to her mind. It was as if a shadow had been drawn across the sun. There was no cloud in the sky and yet the shadow remained.

I shall never forget that walk to my dying day. We strolled along the busy Saturday streets as if it was the most ordinary walk in the world. The odd look faded from Janet's face and she smiled at the children and bent down to stroke a cat. My spirits rose again and when we saw a policeman on the other side of the street I was tempted to cry out to him: here she is! I've found her! Call off the search! It was strange to think that the girl they were all looking for was walking along by my side. But nobody recognised her. She was a pale, pretty little thing, like hundreds of others, and she was wearing the little blue and white frock that hung on the rail in many a multiple store that summer.

I seemed to be split in two. One half of me was singing for joy. The other was oppressed with an overwhelming sense of urgency and of apprehension, such as one might feel if one knew someone was bleeding to death and doubted whether help would come in time. She didn't seem to want to hurry; she was tired, but walking quite well. I reasoned with myself: nothing could possibly happen; she was in my care; I wasn't going to leave her for one instant, not till I could leave her with my father and of course he would know immediately what to do.

We came to the shops near home and she stopped to look in the windows.

'Oh look! Isn't that the dairy lady?' she cried. 'I wonder if she's seen me. Do you think she might remember me? It's such a long time ago, isn't it? Such a very very long time ago.'

'Yes, love,' I replied. 'It's a long time ago.'

I pulled her gently away. The vacant stare was coming

back again. The sun still blazed from the cloudless heavens, but the dark shadow deepened.

We turned the corner into our road. She was lagging now, leaning heavily on my arm. Only a minute now, I said to myself; just let me get her to Dad, just let me hand her over to him. I gritted my teeth and plodded on.

We came to within a yard of the entrance. And then I stopped still with horror. The big glass doors were propped open, as always on fine days. And somebody was coming out between them. Somebody who wasn't walking; somebody who was manipulating a wheel-chair. It hadn't occurred to me for one moment that Caroline might be going for her little airing again. And even then I thought only of the shock that Janet would receive, not of the shock it would be to Caroline. I ought to have grabbed Janet, swung her round, hurried her away. But my reactions never were terribly quick, and today my mind was sorely overburdened. I was seconds too late, and in seconds it was all over.

At the very moment when Caroline was negotiating the low step that she usually managed so skilfully, she must have caught sight of Janet. And of course she hadn't known whether Janet was alive or dead. She gave a terrible cry. Her hands shot up to cover her eyes. The chair ran out of control, careered across the pavement, bounced off the kerb in the space between two parked cars and sped on into the roadway. I leapt forward to try and save her, but Janet was on the outside of the pavement and she got there first.

There was a heavy lorry coming from one direction and a stream of cars from the other. They were going at fair speed. The parked cars were blocking their vision in any case and they hadn't a moment of warning. There were screams and shouts and grindings of brakes and sickening crashes of metal against metal. It seemed to last for eternity. Something caught me hard on the thigh and sent me flying against the kerb. I picked myself up and looked around.

The road was a shambles. There were cars at all angles, moving ones crashed into parked ones, parked cars themselves pushed up on to the pavement. And in the midst of it all the great lorry was straddled right across the road, bending a lamp-post on one side, crushing a car on the other. Drivers were jumping out and running forward, windows were being flung up, people were rushing from everywhere.

I saw a bright red patch against the grey tarmac; but it wasn't blood; it was the cushion from Caroline's chair. And I caught a glimpse of something blue and white. But the people surged round and hid it from my view. And I heard a woman's loud cry:

'There's two of them! And one's a cripple!'

She broke out into great hiccuping sobs.

I pushed my way through the thickening crowd. At the side of the lorry a big man who looked like the driver was kneeling down, bending over something. It was a little crumpled heap with one of the arms flung out and the head twisted sideways at an angle never seen in life. The big grey eyes were open and they looked up into the sunshine with an empty stare and the slightly parted lips were drooping at the corners.

They say I went clean out of my mind. They say I fell on my knees beside her and banged my head against the hard surface of the road; that I raved and stormed when they put the body in the ambulance and tried to get in too, and that it took three men to hold me back. I don't remember it at all. But I think I did hear someone say that she'd been killed instantly; she'd taken the full force of the side of the lorry when the driver swung round in his frantic attempt to avoid Caroline, and it had broken her neck.

It was Caroline who lingered some days in a heavy coma. She'd been pitched out of the chair on to her head. She never regained consciousness, but something within her must have clung to life; she didn't want to die. I can remember my parents' sad relief when at last the waiting at her bedside was over. And I can remember the moment when I told them how I had found Janet. I can still see my mother's face with the tears streaming down it and feel the warmth of my father's arms around me.

That was nearly three months ago.

Things have happened since, of course. I got my expected Lower Second degree and I went for an interview with the chemical company and they offered me a fair enough job to start with and good prospects of promotion. And instead of Brian coming to us, I went down to Wales to stay with him, but the visit wasn't a success. Somehow or other I didn't feel like talking to him about Janet, but he misunderstood completely. He told me he'd always thought she was rather a silly little thing and not the sort of wife for me at all. And he kept producing glamorous college girls for my inspection, and altogether I was very glad to be home again. My mother was very sympathetic at first, but after a while she too began to drop broad hints about my taking an interest in other girls, and it was my father with whom I found it easiest to talk.

He blamed himself bitterly for his misjudging of Caroline. He had never imagined her capable of such viciousness and he begged my forgiveness. I told him every detail I could remember of how Janet had been when I brought her home that day and he said he was afraid that hers would have been a very stunted life, hemmed in by fears and phobias. She hadn't the basic mental stamina to withstand the series of shocks that life had dealt her; they'd have left their mark for ever. I asked whether she had run under the lorry to try and save Caroline and he said he thought she probably had; it was a very fundamental instinct, even with someone who had tried to kill you, but he thought there was a strong suicidal impulse there too.

'I'm glad you were bringing her back to me,' he said. 'It's some little comfort to know that was what you wanted to do.'

He never says brightly: oh, you'll get over it. He never asks if I've met any other girls. But of course he knows I will feel differently some day. And I know that too. I'm young and strong and I may have sixty years of life ahead. I shan't mourn for Janet all that time. But I can't help mourning now. It's as if there's a desert around me, filled with a great ache of nostalgia that nothing seems to ease. I see her so often: coming round a street corner, jumping on a bus, disappearing into a shop.

Of course it isn't Janet. Of course it's only one of the hundreds of pale pretty girls in the little blue and white frocks that hang on the rail in all the multiple stores this year. But sometimes when it gets very bad I go and call on Gabriel, who's taken over Lesley's old flat now and who has decided to be respectable and is going back to college to finish his degree.

He gives a loud groan when he sees me at the door and slaps his forehead and cries:

'Christ! Here's Romeo again!'

But he always pulls me in, and throws me a cigarette and brews coffee and then flings himself on his bed and says: 'All right. Therapeutic session is about to begin.'

And he listens patiently to all I have to say and answers all my questions about Janet again and again: how he pulled her out of the water, how he stripped off his shirt to wipe the worst of the damp and muck off her; and made her jump about to keep warm; and marched her quickly back to his room and poured brandy and hot sweet tea into her. And then I ask him: was she frightened all the time? Didn't she smile sometimes? Didn't she sometimes sing to herself in the way I'd heard her do?

I know I'm a sentimental idiot. I know these are just not the sort of things one ought to keep talking about. But somehow with Gabriel it doesn't matter. He never judges. He neither praises nor condemns. There's only one thing I don't ask him, though, and that's for his sake rather than for mine. It's hard to imagine him ever embarrassed, but I really think he would be if I did ask. It wouldn't matter about any other girl, and I'm not over delicate myself; but we just don't talk about Janet in that sort of way. Sometimes I can't help thinking that if he'd left her alone she might have more easily regained her mental balance. For all her flirtatious ways she was a very innocent and rather prudish little thing and Gabriel can be very crude.

But what does it matter now? She's dead and will never be found again. And he's a good friend and is trying his damnedest to pull himself up off his beastly dope. At least he never did that to her. He swears he didn't and I believe him. And sometimes when I go over it all in my mind, all the months since Janet came to live with us, I feel that we were all of us responsible for her death and that Gabriel was the only one who did not fail her.